COURT OF ROGUES

An Urban Fantasy

ANN GIMPEL

CONTENTS

COURT OF ROGUES

MAGICK AND MISFITS SERIES, BOOK ONE

An Urban Fantasy

By

Ann Gimpel

**Tumble off reality's edge into a twisted world
fueled by myth and magick**

Copyright Page

BOOK DESCRIPTION, COURT OF ROGUES

Urban fantasy and slow burn romance wrapped into a serial that will keep you up reading long into the night.

Strange bedfellows rock worlds.

Reluctant recruit to the nines, I became Faery's regent by default. Sure, I was next in line for the throne, but I never believed Oberon and Titania were gone for good until first a decade rolled by, and then two, and then ten.

They'll never be back, and the land is mourning. Or pissed. It's hard to tell which, and I'm not sure what difference it makes. I split my time between Faery and Earth searching for a way to mend the rift that's killing my realm. I haven't made much progress. Time is running through the glass, mocking my paltry efforts.

A sultry Witch is barely a blip on the radar. So what if she counts cards in the casino I run on Earth and makes my pit boss a little nuts? Out of the blue, she spits out the unbelievable, and I discover she's not a Witch after all. A glamour hid her Fae-Sidhe blood so well, she'd fooled me.

Her mixed blood is an affront. By rights, I should haul her before the Court to face justice. She understood the chance she took revealing herself to me, and her offer to join forces is tempting, but it could cost me my throne.

Some risks are worth the price. If I cross the line, there'll be no going back.

Covers play a big role in my creative process. I saw a set of covers featuring a badass Fae prince a while back and bid on them. Unfortunately, someone had a faster Internet connection than me, so I didn't end up with them. But everything comes out as it should because I found another cover I liked even better: the one on this book.

I've always been fascinated with the Otherworld. The faeries' ancestral home goes by many names. It's called *Annwn* in Welsh mythology and *Avalon* in Arthurian legend. In Irish mythology it's referred to as *Tír na nÓg, Mag Mell,* and *Emain Ablach.* Irish myths also feature a place called *Tech Duinn*, where the souls of the dead gather.

But I digress. My vision is a world where mortal and faery collide.

You, my readers, will let me know how well I managed it.

CHAPTER ONE, CYN

The door to my cramped office slapped against its stops, rattling the frosted glass blazoned with Jedediah Rolfson, General Manager, Lady Luck Casino. The gilt lettering had faded, but everyone in the gaming house knew who I was and where to find me. Of course, Jedediah isn't my true name. Names hold immeasurable power. Even if mortals had been able to pronounce my real one, I'd never, never give them that sort of leverage over me.

My door was still vibrating. A knock would have been nice. Respectful, even, but manners had passed most mortals by. Fueled by irritation, my power simmered so close to the surface it took an effort to rein it in. No need to turn around to identify the man who'd disturbed what passed for peace in this place.

"What is it, Rudy?" I still hadn't swiveled my chair to face him.

"How'd you know it was me?" he demanded.

Because I can smell you, idiot...

I did twist then. The motion of my big body forced the ratty leather chair around almost as an afterthought. Stick-straight black hair fell across Rudy's face, and his white shirt was rolled to the elbows. His usual dark pants were rucked up over the tops of battered leather boots. He looked more like a kitchen knave than a pit boss—an underfed kitchen knave who'd stopped growing as a teenager. I made a point of hiring oddballs —freaks and losers. They weren't in a rush to use Lady Luck as a steppingstone for something better.

Angling a pointed look his way, I growled, "Never mind how I know things. What's gone wrong?" I snapped my fingers in the vain hope he might hurry things up.

He squeezed his bloodshot dark eyes shut for a count of two before opening them. "That infernal twit who counts cards is back."

Many patrons count cards, but only one had posed a challenge recently. Interest flickered as I constructed an image of the leggy red-haired Witch with an iridescent nimbus of power floating around her. "You mean the woman?"

"Of course I mean the blasted woman." A touch of

his Russian accent slipped through. "She's the only one who's been able to beat our system."

"What exactly were you hoping I'd do?"

Color stained his sallow cheeks. It was such an unusual response, I delved into his mind and helped myself to his thoughts. Mortals were quite the superficial lot. Culling through their secrets saved me a lot of time.

"Well?" I snapped my fingers again, more out of frustration than actual hope it would move Rudy off the dime.

"Maybe you can tell her to leave." He drew himself up to his full five-foot-eight-inch height, but it didn't have the desired effect. He wanted me to respect him, to back his play, but I'd seen the whole sorry charade in his puny mind. He'd chased the Witch out the last time she stopped by the casino, but he'd also done his damnedest to fuck her.

She'd lured him with a fine set of tits, and then hexed him. Even though he had no concept of what she'd done, her sneaky spell had rendered him impotent. I smothered a chuckle. Witchy charms had a shelf-life. Eventually his little johnny would stand up and salute again, and—

A muted crash came through the audio on one of many screens I'd had mounted so I could see the entire gaming house. Not that I needed them, but they looked good and avoided explanations about how I knew jack concerning the brawl in the basement lounge. The patrons had no idea I spied on them—until I turned them over to the authorities for cheating the house. I've been called a lot of names since I was suckered into taking on this thankless job. So far, I've maintained my cool.

Eventually, though, some hapless mortal will find himself skewered by Fae magic. They'll beg for mercy, for the compassion of a human court, but it will be too late. Mortals never leave Faery unless we release them, not intact, anyway. Those who break free end up in institutions.

"Jed?" Rudy prodded.

"Yeah. Yeah. On my way." I flowed out of my seat. If Rudy weren't hovering in my doorway, I'd have teleported four floors down. Meanwhile, the ruckus was escalating amid the crash of breaking glassware.

"The thieving card counter?" Rudy's gaze skittered away.

"Is that why you're still standing there?" I made shooing motions with both hands. "Christ. Strap on a set. Get moving. I have bigger problems."

The color that had stained his face turned an ugly tomato shade before he spun and pelted down a nearby stairwell mumbling in Russian. He thought I'd never hear him, but he was whining about the fight that had broken out not being on his floor. If it were, the Witch would have beat a hasty retreat.

A snarl of frustration burbled past my throat. I'd never been able to pound the whole team player concept down everyone's throats. Rudy had risen to pit boss because he was honest—and loyal. Maybe it was too much to expect him—or any human in my employ—to show any initiative beyond the basics.

He didn't like me, but then none of the staff did. They sensed I was different, couldn't put their fingers on why that was, and felt uncomfortable in my presence.

Good. I'd never lift a finger to alter their instinctive dread of me.

The day humans can lounge in front of Fae royalty—never mind how far we've fallen—is the day for me to retire to the *Dreaming* and never resurface. A quick glance at the monitor reassured me the brawl was in full swing. No one would notice an unorthodox entrance, so I hopped on an enchanted conduit and emerged in the largest of five gaming halls in a blaze of light.

Muted light, but it still would have given someone pause. Not here, though, and not now. What looked like a motorcycle gang—leather and tatts and piercings—had faced off against a bunch of Asian street hoods who fancied themselves a modern-day version of the mob.

Ha! Bugsy and Al, two of my old buddies, would have laughed until they puked at the comparison. They'd understood how to be badasses because they'd borrowed liberally from Faery. Much of their wickedness never saw the light of day; they were too smart to reveal themselves, and I'd sworn them to silence. Most mortals wouldn't honor such a bond, but they did. They had no idea what I was, but they'd absorbed my lessons like mother's milk. I crossed a few lines—eh, more than a few—by teaching them gruesome ways to inflict pain and death. Even then, my kingdom was on its way out. What were a few more broken rules?

Turned out flaunting Fae law held a price beyond measure, but I'm getting ahead of things.

No one noticed me as I crunched over broken glass, my fury growing at the senseless destruction. The acrid stench of piss merged with the coppery tang of blood. If I didn't establish control over the situation, this room wouldn't be usable for a few days.

Unacceptable. The tables in this gambling hall raked in better than $50,000 a night.

Grunts and curses rained around me as men punched and knifed one another. I sent magic spiraling out, hunting for the telltale bite of metal. Lady Luck had a no-firearms-or-knives rule, and a metal detector sat at the main entrance. It netted us an impressive array of weapons that we stashed in a safe and turned over to the cops once a week.

Yeah. That's right. Bring a gun or a shiv into my club,

and you have to petition the cops to get it back. Works great if the piece is legal, but most of them weren't. Ever since I'd established that brilliant bit of policy, we hadn't seized too many of them.

I'd made it to the front of the large hall. Not a dealer or croupier in sight. Either they were hiding in the shadows, or they'd fled at the first hint of trouble. I'd deal with that later. They were supposed to alert someone like Rudy. Or me. I employed half a dozen pit bosses who rotated through the club.

I'd heard from Rudy, but not about this mess.

Someone catapulted into me from the side brandishing a knife. I punched him squarely in the neck, and he dropped like a stone. Shouts told me I'd made someone happy by knocking out one of their enemies. Another dude decked out in black leather rushed me from the back. I knew he was coming, but I let him think he was getting away with something.

I swear, mortals' intelligence has been on the wane for the past hundred years. If Shit For Brains had any at all, he'd have recognized a dead-to-the-world five-year-old would have heard him bearing down on me. Timing is everything. I turned at the precise moment to hit him with a one-two combo to the gut and heart. I might have killed him, but I didn't care.

Once he was squealing and twitching at my feet, I cupped my hands around my mouth and amplified my voice with magic laced with you'd-better-do-what-I-say-or-your-days-will-be-numbered compulsion.

"Stop. Right Now." Three little words. No need to repeat them.

A slow lazy smile formed, stretching my face into an unaccustomed configuration. Yay me. I still had it. Everyone had frozen in place.

"Excellent," I went on, smooth as melted butter. "Everyone get the fuck out of here except your top dogs. Take the fallen with you."

As the crowd cleared, shuffling toward the door, another of my pit bosses scuttled to my side and cleared her throat. "Sorry, boss," Tatiana mumbled. "I went to find you, but your office was empty."

Kind of like your head.

I'd learned to squelch comments like that long ago. Mortals were notoriously thin-skinned, and Tatiana reeked of fear. She hadn't pissed herself, but it had been nip-and-tuck. Her blonde hair was in an updo, and her skin pale under heavy makeup. She would have been pretty without all the war paint. Blue eyes, her best feature, were framed by thick lashes, and she wore Lady Luck's standard employee uniform: white shirt and black pants. Most of the shirts carried the Lady Luck logo, a phoenix sinking into a crater.

The symbolism escaped everyone except me, and I'd never been in a sharing mood when it came to questions like, "What's that mean, boss?" Besides, even if I told them it represented Faery's decline, they'd have thought I'd had too much to drink.

Meanwhile, four men had moved closer, but not too close. Like I said, I make humans nervous.

"Yeah?" One narrowed his eyes. "What'd you want us for?"

I nailed him with my gaze. I employ a glamour. It smooths the points of my ears and makes my eyes appear blue, rather than a mix of silver and gold with coppery centers. For the slightest of moments, I let it slip a notch, just a hint of a blur.

The dude rubbed his eyes. "Shit. Drunker than I thought." His words were slurred.

It was tempting to display more of what I really was. I shrugged it off. No point in making him yearn for the impossible. He'd be drawn to my deviant beauty. More than drawn. He'd twist himself into a pretzel for one more peek. If I'd wanted a lackey, sure, but I had other plans for him and his partners in crime.

"You have two choices," I told the men who were shifting from foot to foot as they looked mostly at the floor. "Grab mops and buckets and clean up the mess you made."

"Or?" One tried for a sneer, but didn't quite manage it.

"Or I hold you here and call the cops. Property

damage is a felony. Bet you've had a few of those already."

I rocked back on my heels, waiting. Tatiana had drawn closer to me, not because I was warm and fuzzy, but because the thugs made her even more nervous than I did.

"Big talk. How are you planning to keep us from leaving?" Shit For Brains Number Two asked.

I swept an arm wide. "I don't have to. You're all on camera. I give the cops the feed and voila." I dusted my hands together. "I'm sure they know you already."

"We'll clean," he gritted out.

"It would go faster with more of us," another pointed out.

"Probably so, but I don't want 'more of you' in here," I told him. "While we're on that little topic, you and your gang members are barred from Lady Luck from here on in."

The one who'd said his life would be simpler with drones to order about drew himself up. "You can't do that, man."

"The hell I can't," I retorted and turned to Tatiana. "Show these fellows where the cleaning supplies are and oversee the work. They don't leave until you're satisfied they've done a good job."

Her blue eyes widened. "Erm. Maybe the head of janitorial would be better for that."

"He might be," I agreed, trying for an amiable tone, "but I assigned this job to you."

Something in my voice told her arguing was pointless. She'd run at the first whiff of fighting. That story about coming to find me had been pure fabrication. She rolled her shoulders back, barked, "Follow me," and loped across the expanse of parquet flooring.

After a pause a shade too long for my liking, the men turned to follow her. Just so there'd be no misunderstandings later, I called after them, "Don't even think about hassling her. If you do, I'll find out."

I left it there. No need to spell out what I'd do to their sorry, shitty asses if they made a grab for Tatiana's tits or any other part of her. I retreated to one side and wrapped myself in shadows. I wouldn't remain long, only until the cleanup project was underway.

I hadn't realized I'd clenched my hands into fists, and I uncurled my fingers one by one. Damn it, anyway. Everything was broken—and I didn't mean in this gaming room. I was here, straddling worlds, to mend what I could, but I hadn't made much progress.

Or any if I were honest.

Aye, and when I start lying to myself, I'm done for, a patronizing inner voice spouted off.

I wasn't the source of the original damage. It could be traced directly to the Fae court, who'd decided it would be a grand idea to kick Faery's gates open to mortals a century ago. Not that any of us ever cared about humans. We've always held them in contempt, but we wanted their money.

They'd done a bang-up job stripping their world of everything salable and grown filthy rich in the process. My kinsmen are drawn by gold—and I'd be lying if I said it didn't sing to me as well. We all love wealth, which is strange since our creature needs are taken care of in Faery.

At first, around the end of the 1800s, everything appeared to be going smoothly. We provided something not unlike a circus attraction for the well-heeled. One element none of us had reckoned on was Faery herself. Our land is alive, and she rebelled at the presence of those without power. Not right away, but when it happened the backlash was swift, sure, and brutal...

Buckets clattered as they rolled across the faux wooden floor. Some establishments have carpet. Not mine. For just this reason. My impromptu work crew dug in. Two men looked as if they'd never seen a mop before, but after Tatiana taunted them for being inept dicks, they shaped up.

I heard cheers from the strip show one floor up. No reason for me to stay here. I'd have it out with the dealers and croupiers at the all-staff meeting tomorrow afternoon. Tucking my hands into my pockets, I strolled through a wall, angling until I intersected a stairwell.

Rather than naming the deserters, perhaps I'd be better served reiterating club policies to everyone.

The more I considered it, the better I liked my idea. I'd gin up something and have everyone e-sign it. I started to head for the floor show. Getting a gander at bouncing breasts and shaved pussies always settled my mind. Or diverted it, anyway. My cock thickened where it was tucked into my trousers, and I curled my fingers around it, enjoying sensation as it skittered through me.

Sex served as a reminder of the Witch. My cock grew more distended as I remembered her striking face and generous curves. To hell with the dancers in the lounge. I wanted the Witch—up close and personal.

If she was still in Lady Luck, I'd weave a lust spell, make her see only me. My errant member twitched against my fingers. "Yes, yes," I told my sidekick. "She'll want you so much, she won't be able to contain herself."

Rudy managed the blackjack and poker tables. A magnet for card counters, they spanned two rooms on the second floor. I couldn't do much about my erection. It would be as useless as attempting to stuff a genie back into a bottle, so I crafted a diversion spell from my waist down. It would draw eyes away from the tented-out front of my pants.

I bounded into the nearest chamber, gratified by the small noises that verified Lady Luck was making money.

Chips clicking, dealers calling for bets, and cries of delight as patrons raked in cash.

Rudy sidled up to me. "How'd it go?"

"It's handled. How about your assignment."

He screwed his face into an angry mask, adding ten years to his grizzled appearance. "I tried, but I'm not getting anywhere near that bitch ever again. She did something to her blackjack dealer."

"What do you mean, did something?" I added a jot of magical coercion to my question.

"He's not right. Won't look at me. Won't answer me."

Damn my eyes, it sure sounded like a hex. "Is she still at his table?"

Rudy nodded. "I told the dealer not to authorize payout, but—"

"Never mind. I'll take it from here."

"Thanks." For once, Rudy looked cowed, and embarrassed. Like most men, admitting defeat is right up there with swallowing glass shards.

The Witch wasn't in this room, so I crossed the hall and walked into the other one. The feel of her power smacked me mid-chest. Witch magic smells delightful. Aged whiskey and wildflowers with a touch of blood to blend everything together. This witch was old. I could tell from her scent and the extent of her power. It oozed from her and had wrapped around the dealer in visible strands.

Oberon's balls. She didn't need to count cards. She had the dealer in thrall. What did she think she was? A fucking Vampire? Whatever game she was running, she could damn well take it elsewhere.

I strode across the big room with its colorful tables. Horse races played on big screen televisions lining one wall. We took a bite out of bets placed on them too. Unlike a mortal, the Witch knew I was coming. I felt her attention, even though her back was turned.

A long skirt swirled around her sandal-clad feet. Made of a pale green sheer material, it offered tantalizing glances of long legs and made it clear she hadn't bothered with underwear. An equally sheer tunic made of silver fabric embroidered with violet runes covered her from shoulder to hip. Her shapely arms were bare. She told the dealer to hold up—in Gaelic—and he complied. I knew damn good and well Hector didn't speak Gaelic. He's Native American from a local reservation.

How deep in trance did she have him, anyway, that he responded to commands in a foreign tongue?

Slowly, tantalizingly, she twisted until she faced me, upper body first, followed by a two-step motion that bought her hips around. Her eyes were a pale, clear green, her face a study in perfection with high, slanted cheekbones, a regal forehead, and a strong chin.

When she smiled and ran her tongue over her lush

lower lip, I dropped a hasty ward around myself. She could dupe a mortal—snare them in her spells—but I was Fae, and my interest in fucking her had staged a dramatic retreat.

The Witch angled her head to one side, still giving me come-hither vibes. "I know what you are," she purred.

Her words tossed still more cold water on my arousal. "Aye, and I know what ye are as well, Madame Witch," I growled back in Gaelic. "Get out of my casino."

Her full lips formed a pout. "You're no fun." Her magic intensified, pummeling my warding.

My control snapped and I grabbed her upper arm, squeezing hard. "Where is your coven? I will return you, as is my duty for any renegade Witch." I'd stuck to Gaelic, and an archaic form at that. Zero chance of anyone understanding it—other than Witchy-gal.

"No need to get tetchy." She yanked her arm, but I held fast.

"Your coven?" I added a whopping heap of compulsion to my query.

Her face twisted in pain, and I had a momentary twinge of conscience for forcing her. "Don't have one," she ground out.

Her reply had been true, but it shocked me. "Covens

are a requirement," I lectured. "After the Witch uprising of 1943—"

A violent twist jerked her arm out of my grasp. "Don't lecture me on my own history," she hissed. "I'm...different."

"We all are, sweetheart," I told her tartly. "Misfits attract magic."

Her lips twitched into half a smile. "Hate to admit it, but that's catchy."

Fuckity-fuck. She was still trying to con me. "Yeah. Now beat it. And don't come back."

"But I need the money." Her pouty look was back.

"Not my problem, darling. Turn tricks. Get an honest job. Before you go, release my dealer from whatever you did to him."

"If I do, will you hire me?"

The question came out of left field, leaving me dumbstruck. Luckily, a loss for words never lasts long. I started to say hell would freeze over before I'd offer her work, but something stayed my tongue.

"Show up here at five tomorrow afternoon. We'll talk about it."

She tilted her chin and ran her gaze from my toes to my head. Something about her direct stare got me going all over again, even through my warding.

"Good enough." She nodded and walked to the dealer. Reaching into his pants pocket, she withdrew a charm, breathed on it, and we both watched it disintegrate into motes of light.

I eyed the dealer. He still stood motionless, a dreamy expression in place. "Get rid of the other ones too," I told her.

Breath swooshed from her mouth. "I was getting to them. Can't hurry these things or he might turn into the village idiot."

Village idiots predated medieval times, so I asked, "How old are you?"

"Never ask a lady her age," she retorted and retrieved two more charms. By the time they were dead, the dealer was starting to look more like a man and less like a puppet.

She regarded him and spoke a few words before turning to me. "There. Give it a few and he won't remember a thing about any of this. See you tomorrow." Her hips swung enticingly as she strode away.

"What's your name?" I called after her.

"You'll find out tomorrow. When I complete the employment application," she replied in mind speech, not bothering to turn around.

I was still sorting how a Witch had mastered telepathy, not a skill native to their magic, when the dealer made a grunting noise. "Boss. What happened? I feel...off."

"Take a break," I told him. "Back to your table in fifteen."

Without waiting for more questions, I walked out of the card room. It was only an hour from closing time. I could skip the rest of tonight's never-ending drama and slip into Faery. My magic needed a boost, and my mind a rest. The mortal world dragged at me, drained my essence, and made me long for an earlier time.

One before we'd opened our doors to humankind.

CHAPTER TWO, CYN

I took the nearest staircase and just kept on walking after I passed the basement. No one without magic could even see this part of the stairs, but they led through one of many gateways into my realm. One thing we did during the years we curried favor with mortals to lighten their wallets was escorted them into Faery. It was very cloak and dagger, blindfolds and all. Plus we carved little holes in their memories and dropped broad hints we were traveling through mirrors.

What a crock. Mirrors have never led into Faery, and I hope a passel of humans have dealt with serious injuries trying to force their way through glass.

The subtle pressure change that presaged leaving Earth for Faery buffeted me. Damn, it was welcome. Inhaling deeply, I shed my glamour. It's not exactly a power pig, but keeping it in place hour after hour takes a toll. No place smells quite like my domain. It's a cross between spring in the forest and the salt tang of a restless sea. You only get seasons in Faery if you choose. The land is accommodating like that.

Small sounds filled my ears from the creatures, large and small, who called Faery their home. Pausing to let the experience wash over me was hard to resist, but I pressed onward. I'd stop once I reached the castle. Spanning three hilltops, Dubrova Castle had provided a home for Fae royalty since the dawn of our time, which predated the beginnings of human reckoning by thousands of years.

A unicorn cantered past, golden horn glittering in the westering sun. I hailed him, but he didn't slow down. Usually, they're quite chatty, so his snub surprised me. The sun never actually sets here. Instead, it hangs suspended on the horizon until Faery gives the order and drags it back across the sky to begin its transit once again. Sometimes the process takes a few hours, other times a few months.

Oberon and Titania used to be our link to the land, but they're gone. No one knows where. I've always believed the land is mourning for them, but that might be over-the-top sentimentality. Regardless, Faery hasn't been the same since mortals came to visit and our regents left.

The two events were concurrent in time.

The king and queen never warmed to the idea of humans in our midst. They made their displeasure known, but none of us thought they'd pick up and leave. Even after they did, we assumed they'd return. They still might. A hundred years is nothing for us, but with each passing month, my expectations waned. Titania had dropped in from time to time. She'd never stayed long enough to have much of a conversation, but her visits had ceased abruptly fifty years ago.

Had Faery's king and queen made another life for themselves in some distant land? Adopted new subjects —more compliant ones—and written us off?

Eh, it didn't matter. Dubrova's turrets popped up on the horizon, followed by the rest of the imposing structure as I climbed toward it. Built of magic and stones mined from the sea, its walls were iridescent. Their pastel shades glowed in the fading rays of the sun. A crowd was gathered at the bottom of broad graceful steps on the far side of the moat. For once, the portcullis was down.

The gate's position gave me pause since it was never down. Were we under attack from somewhere? The resident serpents, cousins to dragons, swam lazily in the moat's turquoise waters, their black triangular heads bobbing above the surface. They didn't appear concerned, and they were quite the gossip mongers.

In all of Faery's storied history, no enemy had breached our barriers. The moat and portcullis were for show. The Fae who'd built them had a penchant for the pomp and circumstance of an earlier era. One that embraced showy displays of power. Those Fae had long since retired to the *Dreaming*. I visited occasionally, but not since I ended up running Lady Luck.

Since I'd have to employ enchantment anyway to get past the portcullis, I jumped skyward, intent on landing in the midst of the crowd. Mostly Fae, but I picked a few Sidhe out of the crowd, along with nymphs, satyrs, a herd of unicorns, and two dragons. So this was where the unicorn had been heading in such a rush. The dragons got my blood flowing. They wouldn't have left Fire Mountain if it weren't important. Every once in a while one traded blasts of steam and smoke with the serpents in the moat.

No love lost there, distant relatives or not.

I tumbled to the ground slightly to the left of my target, and hit harder than I would have liked. Not the elegant entrance I'd hoped for, but my pride was small potatoes in the long run. Dusting myself off, I sprang to my feet to cries of my true name ringing sweetly in my ears.

The unicorn who'd galloped past me sidled near and lowered his head, taking care with his horn. The beasts only look whimsical. They can gore a beast twice their size, whinny up a storm while it died, and then eat what they'd killed. "Sorry for not stopping," he neighed.

I patted his neck. "No worries. I was enjoying being home. Earth isn't an especially commodious spot tonight."

"Or ever." The unicorn rubbed his horn up and down my arm in a show of solidarity.

"Good thing he saw you," my cousin Aedan called from across the green. "Saved me from sending someone to tell you to return." Next in line for Faery's throne after me—assuming Oberon and Titania were truly gone for good—he swept a fall of pale hair behind broad shoulders.

I walked over to him, and we touched palms, mixing magics for a moment in greeting. He's shorter than my seven-foot height by a few inches, and more broadly built. The bulk I sport on Earth is part of my glamour. It's only my height that doesn't change. Aedan's usually impeccable garb—leather trousers and vest—were dusty. Rather than his customary sandals, his feet were bare.

A fiery blast from behind me suggested the dragons were growing impatient. They never did wait well. My longed-for rest, where I lounged in my chamber reading books and experimenting with spells, while I mapped out a strategy to deal with the Witch who wanted to work for me, wasn't in the cards. Lucky for me, Fae don't actually require sleep.

I glanced at the growing crowd, hoping someone would offer up clues, but no one did. I've spent enough time among humans to have grown used to their communication style. It's refreshing and direct—one of the few things I respect about them. On the other hand, we Fae pride ourselves on oblique words, dialogue that leaves others guessing. We live forever, and there are so few secrets left to uncover we savor the ones that pop up. After a few minutes had ticked past, I folded my arms across my chest and announced, "I'm going inside."

"But you can't leave," Aedan protested.

"Not much is happening out here," I retorted and turned on my heel, walking quickly to underscore my threat of abandonment.

The dragons launched their bulks skyward amid the clatter of scales. A stray spray of flames set a small bush on fire, but one of the serpents blasted it with water after bugling his displeasure.

"Cynwrigg ap Llyr." Aedan invoked my true name and bowed low, an atypical gesture.

I spun to face him. "I'm not inclined to play games. Either tell me why everyone is gathered, or I'm retiring to my chambers. I'm due back at Lady Luck in a short while, and I am not in a good mood."

One of the dragons, the blue one, skidded in for a landing scant inches from my feet. I angled my gaze his way. If he so much as tossed a cinder onto my boot tops, I'd send him packing.

"How does it happen you left Fire Mountain?" I asked when he appeared just as loathe to speak as everyone else.

Aedan cleared his throat. "The dragons have a problem—" he began.

The dragon sitting in front of me had curled his upper body well off the ground, so his head sat even with mine. His eyes spun like pinwheels, golden with deep-green centers. He opened his mouth, displaying triple rows of razor-sharp teeth with shreds of his last meal still clinging to them.

"Nay," he bugled, drowning Aedan out. "All of you have a problem. Fire Mountain is merely the leading edge."

"Leading edge of what?" I ground out.

"Ye'll recall, Fire Mountain was the first of the magical worlds," the dragon recited in a tone that reminded me of a million-year-old history professor.

"Of course I know that." I kept my tone sharp and businesslike. Dragons were the storytellers of Faery. With any encouragement at all, Blue-Boy would spin this out for hours.

"The dragons' home world will soon be no more," he intoned. Once he'd dropped that bombshell, he waited a few seconds before adding, "If naught changes."

"What? How is that possible?" I pressed for details.

"I was just there." Aedan made a show of trying to dust off his leathers, but all he did was move the dirt around. "The main volcano has gone mad. Rivers of lava are coating the sands."

A hasty search through my memory banks provided information. "Not the first time it's occurred," I reminded my cousin as I pictured the line of fifteen active volcanoes that made up the spine of Fire Mountain's arid, sunbaked world.

"Aye, but three other mountains have joined in. Nothing like it has ever occurred before." Aedan's normally bland expression had shaded to worry with creases in his high forehead and around his silver eyes.

"What are the other dragons doing?" I asked the one in front of me. The other, a green, was still circling overhead bugling like a crazed creature.

"We have taken refuge in the sacred cave. For now. If conditions worsen, we will all come here."

It wasn't welcome news. Dragons had their own world for the best of reasons. They didn't play well with others. Hundreds of them would run rampant through Faery's delicate greenery, artistic pools, and white sand beaches, rendering them unusable. Eh, there might not be hundreds of wyrms, but even fifty of them could dish out incalculable damage. And I knew there were more than fifty dragons filling Fire Mountain's skies.

An unpleasant thought intruded, and I asked, "Has anyone taken a look at the schism?"

Aedan's expression was all the answer I required. "I'll check it," I told everyone, set a conduit built from magic, and left. The schism—a rift in Faery's foundations—had formed soon after our regents left. I always figured it was Faery's rebellion because we'd invited mortals to pass her gates. With Oberon and Titania absent, none of us possessed sufficient power to close the breach.

Not from the Faery side.

It was why I'd opted to spend time on Earth at the urging of Aedan and others in our court. Jedidiah provided a believable front, allowing me to set up shop beyond Faery's gates. The casino was my third venture spread over an eighty-year timespan. It took a few months to whip Lady Luck into shape—because it was a smoking ruin when I took over. Once it was solvent, I returned to hunting for a companion rift on Earth's side of the barrier. I had yet to locate one, but once I did I hoped I'd have better luck containing it. Better was relative since I'd had zero impact from my domain. The land didn't respond to my call, and I'd tried everything I could think of.

Meanwhile, the rift had deepened by perhaps 50 percent during the years I'd sought to cure it. Oberon's blood flows through my veins, but apparently not enough to make a difference.

All lands in Faery are linked. The dragon had said as much when he'd proclaimed we were all doomed. It might be a good argument to gently suggest he and his kin move elsewhere. Not much point in dragging up stakes if your new location is on its way out too.

My thoughts returned to the schism and my current task, which was taking a good hard look at it. If Fire Mountain was melting down, literally, perhaps the agitation wasn't localized. As I sank into the bedrock layers beneath my world, I hoped my hunch had been wrong. Not that I'm given to hyperbole or flights of wild fancy, but neither do I believe in coincidences.

I snapped my fingers; a mage light mounted on a carved staff formed in one hand. Its multihued light danced crazily off limestone walls as I continued my descent. Finally, the bottom rose up to meet me. I should come here more often, but it's not a comfortable spot. Faery's power is thick, as is her revulsion for the Fae sullying her land with human visitors.

A century may have passed, but she has a long memory.

I landed next to a jagged strip cutting through Faery's foundation. It didn't look any wider, so I walked along the verge. And walked. And walked. Not wider, but considerably longer. Returning to my starting place,

I didn't need to trace the rift in its other direction. It had grown, which was all I needed to know.

"I feel your presence, your magic," I told the land. "I respect it, and I am most sorry we displeased you."

Like every other trip I'd made to this spot, silence reigned. If words wouldn't do it, maybe magic was the ticket. I opened my power and reached for Faery's enchantment. The moment of contact rocked me; for a nanosecond I hoped this time would be different, but it wasn't to be. Like an overstretched rubber band, my seeking spell snapped, blasting me in the magical center. Far worse than a slap in the face or a punch to the guts, the shock wave whacked me in a wicked undulating wave that just kept coming. I staggered back a few steps.

Sinking into a crouch, I caught my breath. When I got my feet under me and stood once again, I said, "I am not your enemy. Faery's history flows rich in me. Oberon is gone, and I am regent in his stead. Until he returns, allow me to help you. We need one another. Faery cannot die." I hesitated before adding, "You cannot die. I will not let you. Death is the coward's way out."

I winced. Had I been too blunt?

A low tortured moan rose from the depths of the chasm spreading before me. Followed by another, it broke my heart and my spirit and filled me with hopelessness. Spreading my hands in front of me, I echoed my entreaty. "Let me help you."

The temperature dropped until my breath made clouds in the chilly air, but Faery didn't make another sound. I remained until icicles formed on the rock walls, holding my mind and my magic open. The magic part was risky, given what had happened last time, but I needed to prove my integrity.

Nada.

Whatever I had to offer, Faery wasn't interested. I'd thought the moans were a crack in her veneer, but I'd been mistaken. "It's an open offer," I said at last. "You can always find me."

My magic was slow to respond when I crafted a spell to return to the lands above. It made no sense. I hadn't expended any power standing around.

Had Faery somehow tapped into me and been draining me so quietly I hadn't noticed? The concept chilled me and meant I'd have to take far more care when I returned. Why did Faery need an infusion of anything? The land was ancient beyond reckoning, and it had never required anything from any of us.

Or I didn't believe it had. Oberon might know different. Or Titania.

I thought about it as I traveled upward at perhaps a tenth the velocity of my trip in the other direction. I was still considering what to do next when I oozed through into Faery next to one of the land's many crystalline pools.

Aedan walked through a gash in the air and stood in front of me, an expectant expression his face. "Well?" He spun one hand in a circle.

"Set markers to find me, did you?" I answered his query with one of my own.

"What of it? How is the rift?"

"Much longer."

He pinched the bridge of his nose before commencing to stare at me again. "How much longer, cousin."

"Regent, to you," I snapped. "When's the last time you looked? Did you measure it?"

"Checking on it is your job," he pointed out.

His tone didn't do anything to temper the frustration twisting my stomach into knots. I might not require sleep, but I do need to eat. I turned away, sucked in a breath, and blew it out. I'd gain exactly nothing by lighting into Aedan. When I twisted to face him, I said, "Maybe you'd like to take over on Earth?"

"Wouldn't work," he reminded me. "My energies aren't a good blend with—"

I chopped a hand downward. "I recall well enough. I'm the logical patsy for Earth duty. Perhaps we might parcel out some of my other tasks to compensate for the fact I'm not here as much."

"What happened down there?" He pointed to our feet.

"Nothing." Mentioning the moaning seemed ridiculous, so I changed the direction of our discussion by asking, "Why were so many gathered in front of the castle? I understand why dragons would be there, but nymphs? Sidhe?"

Aedan's grim expression softened. "It's their world too," he said. "Once the dragons arrived, news traveled like lightning." He slugged me in the shoulder. Not hard. More to get my attention than anything else. "Come on."

"Come on, where?"

"Back to inform the others what you found. They're all waiting."

I started to tell him he could do as well as me with that task, but I was regent. Only so much I could avoid. "Take us," I said.

An odd look crossed his face, but he didn't ask after my magic. Good thing. I wasn't about to divulge my suspicions about Faery using me as a fueling station. It would make me sound like a paranoid idiot.

The pool vanished, replaced by the stout timbers and glittering stones of Dubrova Castle. Everyone's eyes zeroed in on me, and I felt the subtle click of my link to all of them, even the damned dragons. That part of Oberon and Titania's magic had transitioned to me after they'd been gone about twenty years.

It was when I'd first suspected they'd never return.

I pushed my shoulders back, painfully aware of how shoddily I was garbed to stand before them as their prince. There'd been no time to change, so I still wore the black pants and white shirt that were *de rigueur* at Lady Luck. It was stupid. No one cared if I wore sumptuous robes or nothing at all.

"The rift has grown," I told the crowd. "Not wider but longer. It shouldn't affect the integrity of Faery's foundations, but we don't want to allow it to grow bigger still." Here was where the rubber met the road. Many eyes were glued on me, seeking direction.

My gaze shifted to the dragons, both on the ground this time. "Return to Fire Mountain. Report in if things worsen."

The blue spread his wings, but I held up a hand. "I do not believe it will come to this, but designate a few small teams of dragons to investigate other worlds where you might settle."

"We're coming here." The green dragon tossed his snout.

"What sense is there in that?" I asked. "If Fire Mountain crashes and burns, Faery won't be far behind. Better to find a spot where you don't have to move again."

The blue puffed smoke. "Good point, Regent. We shall be in touch. You can always check in on us too."

"We shall," I assured him.

Once they'd left, I turned to Aedan. "You've already been there."

He understood my drift. "I will visit the dragons' home world every other day beginning tomorrow."

I held up my palm. He touched it with his own to seal his commitment.

"What can we do?" A tiny fairy with dappled wings and violet hair fluttered near.

"Aye." Another joined her, scarlet wings thrumming with concern. "Dragons are strong. We cannot relocate so easily."

I spread my arms to encompass the group. "We will figure something out. I cannot believe Faery will desert us. Believe in her. In the meantime, be on the lookout for anything unusual magically. Report all incidents to the court."

"What will you be doing...Regent?" A satyr leered at me. The pause before my title told me exactly what he thought about the current state of affairs and my ability to guide us through rough waters.

"Taking care of Faery and all her people—including you." Before I said more, including things I was sure to regret, I executed a leap. The maneuver landed me in front of the castle's imposing front doors. The structure recognized me, allowing access, and I waltzed through its twelve-foot, richly carved entrance.

Aedan caught up before I was halfway across the

great room. "I'll check on the schism too," he reassured me. "Any ideas about chasing down Oberon?"

I shook my head. "Not a one, but I still have to try. We need him. Titania too. Everything is connected somehow. It's like putting a puzzle together and discovering some of the pieces are wrong or missing."

"What do you mean?" he asked as we mounted the stairs. My chambers were on the top floor tucked away in a corner.

"We're missing something," I told him. "I hold the link to Faery's people, but not the one to the land..."

"They were designed to go together."

"Aye, I know. Hence my statement we're lacking something critical."

"Let me know what you need from me." Aedan stopped on his floor and executed a formal bow.

Nodding in return, I continued upward, but guilt nagged. Aedan had said he would check the rift. "Guard your magic when you go below," I called after him. "Something's off down there."

"Got it," drifted back. "Thanks."

No thanks needed, I thought sourly. The other option would be picking up still more pieces if Faery recognized Aedan for the soft touch he was and sucked him dry.

CHAPTER THREE, DARIYAH

I scurried out of Lady Luck after my run-in with Cynwrigg ap Llyr. When I'd told him I knew what he was, he probably figured I knew he was Fae. He'd have been shocked—and worried—I knew his true name. I could see through his glamour too. It had been one of the side benefits of stalking him.

What a striking, gorgeous hunk of a mage he was. Not the burly buffoon he played in his role at the casino. Not at all. Beneath his glamour, the Fae was amazing. Pushing seven feet tall, his body was lithe and graceful for its height. Muscles banded across his shoulders and back, winding down his arms. Long legs supported slender hips and a high tight ass that made me itch to get my fingers on it.

His long, lush locks were pale gold. They framed an

arresting face with a high forehead, sculpted cheek-bones, and a square chin. Like all Fae, he was beardless, and the graceful tips of his ears peeked through the cascade of hair.

Even though I was walking quickly, a shot of pure lust swirled through me. I'd wanted Cynwrigg from the moment I laid eyes on him. Wanted him with a single-mindedness that threatened to derail why I was slumming in Lady Luck. I'd brought myself off a hundred times—maybe more—fingers buried deep in my quim, thrusting fast and hard, as I imagined what his cock would feel like taking me from the front, from behind, or with my legs wrapped around his hips after I'd crawled up his body.

And then there was my mouth. I could almost feel him stretching me as I laved his length with my tongue and worked him with my hands. My breath was coming fast, and my nipples had formed stiff peaks.

"Hecate! Save me from myself," I murmured, but of course she didn't answer. She's the goddess of Witches, and I am so not a Witch.

The motion of my thighs rubbed my slick labia together as I trotted along, adding fuel to my lust and making it impossible to think. I needed to concentrate, plot out my next moves. I hadn't expected tonight would be my first actual confrontation with Cyn. And I sure as hell hadn't planned on asking to sign on to his payroll, but he had the ability to ban me from Lady Luck. And seal the ouster with runes that would alert him if I crossed the lintel.

I couldn't let that happen, so I'd gone with my instincts and asked him to hire me. In a full-on skirmish, my magic might overshadow his, but I wasn't positive of that, and I couldn't risk it. Not yet.

I'd been unnerved when he broke into my private party with the dealer. I'd figured on a run-in with the wimpy, oversexed Russian who couldn't stay away. Even after I'd cut the nuts out from under his pathetic dick, he hadn't quit ogling me. And I'd given him an eyeful. Even let him catch me in one of the ladies' rooms teasing my clit. I'd figured it was him who'd installed the micro cameras in all the stalls. Or maybe it was just his job to monitor them to make sure no one was stealing from the club.

Damn. This wasn't working. All I could think about was Cyn. Literally. I'd been at Lady Luck almost every night, but I'd taken care to wipe minds so no one remembered me. Tonight, I'd been sloppy because I was preoccupied. My game plan had ground to a halt, and I needed to jumpstart it. The dealer had been a diversion, a way to exercise my magic, take it out for a romp.

A hasty glance around told me I was alone. It was late, past two in the morning, and I'd stuck to quieter streets after leaving the casino. Reno is a godforsaken place; skanky monoliths built out of concrete and steel jut upward like permanent erections.

Needing encouragement to douse the sexual hunger still dogging me, I shook myself from head to toe. The towers looked like spaceships, not dicks. Yeah, that was better. Not as accurate, but so what? A muffled snort startled me. Not so alone as I'd thought I was.

"Hey, bitch."

I smelled stale booze and rank sweat before I saw a man shambling out from between two parked cars. Remnants of the dude he'd once been clung to a tall frame that was going to fat.

This could be over really fast, but I kept walking, speeding up my pace.

"Bitch." He slurred the word, missing the T sound.

I broke into a trot, but he lumbered after me. Eh, we could do this until he fell on his face. He was already wheezing. And then I smelled metal and heard the *snick* of a hammer being drawn back. There's only so much I'm willing to endure at the hands of mortals.

Not in a hurry at all, I turned and faced him. He wasn't expecting me to do anything but run, and he ground to a halt, confusion spreading over his ruined features. Amazing what booze can do to a person. And way faster than heroin.

"Look at me." I netted him in the simplest of spells. Rheumy brown eyes scuttled from side to side before finally settling on my face. "There you go," I told him. "Now, turn around and walk away."

I fully expected him to obey me. Instead, he stood stock still, swaying from foot to foot. Odd. Humans can't resist my commands, but this one didn't show any sign of leaving. The gun was still pointed at my tits. Not a problem. Bullets are an annoyance, but they can't hurt me.

Trying a different tack, I purred, "Put the gun down."

His finger tightened on the trigger about the time I sensed others gliding toward him. Others who weren't human. That explained why the oversized clown facing me hadn't complied with my orders. A quick prod rendered the warding around him visible. At least my desire for Cyn receded as I studied the problem. Thank the goddess for small favors.

Very few magic-wielders inhabit Earth. Something about the warp and weft of the energy here isn't compatible with power. If we remain long, our ability ebbs until it's mostly gone. If you pay heed to legends, some long-standing Earth dwelling mages ended up here because their power never returned.

Two shifters, a Witch—a real one—and a wizard were heading my way. Why had they bothered with the drunk?

"Show yourselves." I spread my hands in front of me, power flickering between them.

"What the fuck?" The mortal stared at me. Fear contorted his features into a Halloween mask. I turned up the lumens on my otherworldly aspects; the acrid stench of piss pricked my nose. Pistol still clutched in one hand, the hapless fool shambled into as close to a run as he could manage. At least the air was cleaner after he left.

"Dariyah." The Witch closed on me. White hair framed her seamed face, but she stood tall, her body not yet bent by age. The shifters morphed into their animal forms, a larger-than-life raven and a red fox. They flanked the Witch like a metaphysical honor guard.

Not much point denying it was me since a truth spell had dropped over my head. To hell with that. Ignoring the Witch's use of my true name, I asked, "Why'd you draw that poor sod into whatever this is?"

"We had to make certain it was you," the wizard replied. Garbed in white robes with a pointed hat and a flowing gray beard, he looked like a reincarnation of Gandalf.

"Your glamour is more difficult to pierce than one that only covers physical traits," the Witch explained as if she were imparting a prime bit of information I didn't already know. I'd picked the Witch veneer to hide behind because it was pretty much bombproof. Pretty much. Apparently not so ironclad when I wasn't on top of my game, but this batch couldn't have figured out what I am. If they had, they'd be chattering like a flock of outraged magpies.

"So if it hadn't been me, that fuckstick would have shot the not-me," I sputtered.

"We would have stepped in." The wizard added a calming patina to his words. I saw a spell floating in the air.

I rolled first one shoulder back and then the other. "Why were you hunting me?"

"We carry a message from Oberon." The Witch switched to a shielded form of telepathy. I don't know why she bothered. We were the only magical creatures in a forty league radius. Except Cyn, and I was damned certain his focus lay elsewhere.

"Tell him I'm not ready to leave yet." I flapped a hand their way. As a mage for hire, if I left now it would void the contract and give Oberon, notorious skinflint that he was, an excuse to stiff me on my fee.

"He says you're done." The wizard was still pumping out calming vibes.

I rounded on him. "I say I'm not."

The raven cawed; the fox made little yipping sounds. I could have dug into their minds, but I wasn't in the mood.

"He figured you'd be stubborn," the Witch cut in. "He was most clear. If you back away now, he'll honor half your agreed-upon contract amount."

I looked askance at her. "And if I don't?"

"Then you get nothing," The wizard sounded almost cheerful. I doubled up a fist and considered driving it into his face.

Anger bubbled, burning a trail through me. Four against one weren't great odds, but I could take them. As soon as that little tidbit kicked me in the butt, I knew I'd push this puppy as far as I could. Oberon only thought I reported to him. He'd abandoned Faery and his subjects in a snit. Ever since then, he'd hired a succession of spies to keep an eye on his erstwhile realm. I was merely the most recent in a long string. Everyone else had quit, and now I knew why.

What happened next wasn't the smartest move I've ever made, but I was steamed. "You tell Oberon this," I snarled. "I shall complete my task. If he refuses to honor his agreement with me, I will tell Cynwrigg everything. He's the *de facto* regent, and he has a right to know."

The four mages had moved into what was clearly a prearranged formation while I talked. I was ready for them, though. I shot the raven out of the air with a blast of earth-tinged air. Before it hit the ground, I locked the fox into a fiery cage. It's squeals were pathetic, but I shut my ears.

Unlike most mages, I control all the elements. Born of a forbidden Fae-Sidhe pairing, I was lucky to be alive. Others like me had been ferreted out at birth—or before

—and dealt with. Mother—the Fae half of things—had kept me safe until I was old enough to manage on my own. I imagine she was still in hiding since whoever brought her to justice would collect a fat purse.

We'd said goodbye hundreds of years before. I'd known I'd never see her again, but I still missed her. It was lonely life when you didn't fit anywhere, and of course Faery was barred to me. I had no idea who my father was. Mother never told me. After a time, I quit asking.

I can ferret out who everyone else's magical parents are, just not my own.

The wizard was edging nearer, a determined expression on his face. The Witch hadn't moved since I'd taken out the shifters. I waggled my fingers at both of them. "What'll it be? I leveled the field nicely. Two against one are no odds at all. Choice time ends in five seconds. Five. Four. Three. Two..."

The Witch punched out in a shimmery red haze. Apparently Wizard-Boy decided he didn't want to face me alone. He shook a fist my way. "You'll be sorry."

"Quaking in my boots, buddy. Quaking, I tell you." By the time I was done laughing, he was gone.

The fox was still screaming; the bird was still out cold. I took pity on them and dismantled the power holding them prisoner. Casting nervous glances my way, the fox shifted back to his human form. Of course, his clothing lay in shreds, but he didn't pay it any heed. Scooping the bird into his arms, he teleported to points unknown leaving me scratching my head.

Why had Oberon pulled the plug? I was well within the timeframe of our agreement. Jobs weren't so easy to come by, not ones that actually let me be who I was. I've never done well flipping burgers or being a secretary. The king of Faery was an enigma for sure. Maybe he'd pulled this stunt with all his hired spies—to avoid paying them. Maybe. No amount of pondering would yield the answers I needed.

My apartment wasn't far. A basement walkup, it offered easy access to magical channels leading away from Earth and an equally ready way to replenish my power. The adrenaline rush was fading, and I felt stupid. Kicking Oberon's lackeys halfway back to Faery had been satisfying as fuck, but woefully shortsighted. They'd tell him exactly what I'd said, and Oberon would send new troops after me. More competent ones than this bunch of dipshits had been. I didn't understand how the king still had underlings at his disposal, but it wasn't important.

Yeah, it is, an inner voice spoke up.

Fine. I'd think more on it later. Too weary to bother with keys, magic, or the door to my flat, I flowed through its walls and sucked in the cozy cinnamon and vanilla smell of the place I'd called home for a few months. It was one room with a mattress on the floor in one corner and a computer on a desk in another. The kitchen was separated from the main room by a curtain and was as basic as kitchens came. No problem since I'm not much of a cook. Or one at all.

A tiny bathroom completed my digs. At least they were cheap. Money wasn't a problem. I could knock over an ATM machine whenever I wanted, but I concealed my illegal activities, so they remained strictly under wraps. Preserving a very low profile kept me out of everyone's gunsights—for the most part.

I pulled open the door to my postage-stamp-sized fridge. Two cans of Coke and a cardboard container of leftover Chinese leered back at me. I grabbed one of the Cokes and an energy bar from the cupboard. It tasted like sawdust, but the nutritional data printed on its wrapper promised great things. I had my doubts. Mortals' love affair with turning food into something four times removed from its source ingredients would be the death of them.

Things were already trending that way. The current generation wasn't living as long as the previous one. I blamed what they ate when I thought about it at all. Mortals were the least of my problems. I hunkered into a crouch, back supported by a wall.

I'd leave my lair, trading it for the spot I replenished my power, soon. First, though, I had decisions to make.

Why had I been so obstinate about spying on Cynwrigg? Was it because I'd been hoping for a quick fuck?

That would have been a nice, neat answer. It would have allowed me to pull up stakes and walk away. Unfortunately, things weren't so simple. The Fae fascinated me. The longer I'd watched him, the more intrigued I became until I could barely wait until the next evening and my trip to Lady Luck.

I dropped my head into my hands and rubbed my temples. A brisk *mwroww* snapped my head around. Midnight, the black cat who'd adopted me, strolled across my almost empty room and crawled up my side, digging his claws in along the way. When he got to my shoulders, he draped himself across them, purring up a storm.

I wriggled a hand into position and stroked his soft head. The purring increased, soothing my agitation. "Will you ever tell me how you get in and out?" I asked.

"Mrowwwww."

I chuckled. "Yeah. Didn't think so. Some secrets are worth dying for."

Kitty-Boy was weakly magical, but then most cats are. He'd come with the flat. Been waiting the day I moved in. I'd viewed it as a lovely coincidence, but was it? I'd just accepted the job from Oberon. It was why I'd moved here. No other reason anyone in their right mind would want to live in this godforsaken desert peppered with neon and desperate gamblers certain one more spin of the wheel would fix them up for life.

Midnight had settled in and dozed off, body curved around mine. I took care, was as gentle as I knew how when I probed his feline consciousness. I wanted to be wrong, wanted him to be just a cat who'd lived here before I rented the place, but my suspicions were running high.

Oberon was a sketchy piece of work. From what I'd seen of Titania—and it had only been from afar of necessity—she had scruples, ethics. Two items her husband lacked. My journey through the cat's mind was uneventful, filled with mice and rats and food dishes. I saw humans and a fluffy tabby with kittens. Presumably, Midnight was the proud daddy.

I'd gotten to where I was breathing a big sigh of relief Oberon hadn't sicced the cat on me to monitor my movements when I stumbled across a place that wasn't kitty-like at all. As soon as I found it, I knew exactly what it was. A reflective device to transmit information.

Calm, an inner voice suggested silkily. *Keep calm.*

Breath rattled in and out as I hung on to my temper. I could injure Midnight if I blew a gasket while I was connected to him. This wasn't his fault. He was an innocent pressed into service without his knowledge. I started to withdraw, but held off.

What should I do about the device?

If I destroyed it, Oberon would know I was onto him, but he'd know soon enough anyway. After the Witch and wizard bent his ear about our run-in—and my threat to chat it up with Cyn. Hell, he probably knew already. I liked the cat. Respected him. He was too good to be used like this.

Before I thought it to death, I measured the spot carefully, focused a tiny beam of magic, and neutralized Oberon's beacon. Oblivious, a still-purring Midnight slept on. Excellent. The cat would never know, but Oberon was likely fuming. He'd have felt the moment I clipped through the enchantment powering his one-way mirror. Still treading carefully, I completed my retreat and sealed over evidence I'd ever been there.

Assured the cat was safe, I allowed fury I'd suppressed to rage through me. Even if Cyn didn't fascinate me, Oberon's underhanded efforts to watch my every move pissed me off. Worse than that, I was appalled. And I felt dirty. Like I'd been victimized by some pervert getting his rocks off watching me.

"Don't get mad, get even," I mumbled. Determination edged out anger, winning the day.

I'd tell Cynwrigg everything. He'd have a right to demand my head on a pike for talking shit about his king. And for being a forbidden half-breed. Nothing I could do about what I was. This wasn't about me. Oberon had exited stage left, not precisely lying, but neither was he being forthright about his whereabouts to his subjects.

I knew more or less where he was, and I'd make certain Cyn did as well.

I transferred the cat to my arms, stood, and carried him to the bed. Thinking he might fall in love with the leftover Chinese, I transferred it into a cracked ceramic bowl and left it next to his water dish. By the time I was done, he was on his feet, hunched over the bowl, and eating with enthusiasm.

"Good hunting, boy," I told him and melted through a wall. If things played out as I suspected they would, I'd need all the magic I could lay my hands on. Once I was done topping off my tank, I'd eat and rest.

But not at my flat. It was the first place Oberon would deploy henchmen hunting me. I wasn't worried about the cat. Whoever pursued me would leave as soon as they determined I wasn't there. My best bet would be to remain in the in-between place until it was time to go to Lady Luck tomorrow afternoon.

Spinning a concealment spell, I covered my tracks so well no one could have found me.

❦ 4 ❦

CHAPTER FOUR, CYN

Considering how little I accomplished, the day passed quickly. No one reported anything unusual to the court. I call it a court, but it's more like a council. I preside over all the critical decisions, but a rotating crew of twelve mages serve as delegates. We rely on democratic process these days. One mage. One vote. When Oberon and Titania were in residence, they'd frequently pulled rank, ignoring whatever accord the rest of us had developed. It led to hard feelings, but they'd ruled us forever, and we were used to them.

When I took over as regent, I never felt right standing in front of a group of my peers and telling them it was my way or the highway. I reserved that level of high-handedness for the Lady Luck casino. It needed managing far more than Faery did. Up until recently, Faery hadn't required much of anything at all.

I looked for Aedan before I crossed the barrier back to Earth, but he'd left. Or maybe he had nothing to say and was avoiding me. Not because he didn't like me but because I served as a visceral reminder of the troubles facing us. I didn't blame him. One advantage of Oberon's style was he took care of everything in his own way.

We trusted him to take care of us, maybe not in the same manner we would have, but his bond to Faery and its people had been unbreakable. I still didn't understand how he could have walked out on us, but I didn't expect he'd ever return.

Which meant I'd have to up the ante and figure out where he was. He could parley with Faery, calm the distraught land, and remind her of her job providing a home for all of us.

At least I'd cleaned up, donned fresh clothes, and was ready to pick up the reins at Lady Luck. Hoping nothing else had turned to shit during the hour I'd skated out of there the previous night, I rode a magical conduit to Earth's side of the barrier and mounted the stairs leading to the casino, making certain my glamour was in place. It was just shy of five when I strode into my office expecting either a crowd of staff with issues or a pile of notes—electronic and on paper.

Nothing looked any worse than usual. No one was

standing at my door, waiting impatiently. I snagged my phone out of a drawer and took a quick peek at its contents. The work crew I'd pressed into service had done a decent job. Tatiana said the chamber would be ready to go for tonight's activities.

Rudy and the other pit bosses had filled out the daily tally sheets. Despite the brawl, last night had netted us well over a hundred thousand dollars before expenses. Our breakeven point was forty thousand, so the club was comfortably solvent.

I was just congratulating myself for having escaped unscathed from leaving early when the tantalizing scents belonging to the Witch made my nose twitch. I hadn't exactly forgotten about her, but I hadn't expended any time at all planning for how to deal with her request to work here, either.

Probably just as well. I didn't have to dig too deep to know she'd be nothing but trouble. I'd never be able to trust her with her charms and spells. She'd always be up to something, and I did not need any more on my overflowing plate. The immediate future meant less time at the casino as I upped my game searching for the rift. Witchy-babe couldn't be here without me to supervise. Goddess only knew what havoc she'd wreak.

No need to prepare anything elaborate by way of refusals. This would be a short, sweet no.

She stopped on the other side of my closed door and

knocked. There wasn't any reason to hide magic from her, so I sent a jolt that opened the door. She hovered in the doorway, appearing tentative, but it was only an act. Subservient wasn't part of her character.

"This is the right time, isn't it?" she asked. "If you need me to wait outside, I can."

My magic wasn't the only jolt. Gods, she was even more stunning than I remembered. She'd ditched the sheer clothing for a plain white blouse and long black skirt that clung to her slender waist and the curves of her hips. A simple gold necklace spanned her neck. Red tresses hung to waist level in a cascade of curls, and her green eyes were enhanced with the smallest application of makeup.

"No need to wait. Come on in." I kept my tone gruff to conceal my delight at her presence.

She glided inside and shut the door behind her. When she turned to me, she said, "Thanks for the opportunity."

Oops. Need to head this one off at the pass.

I got to my feet. "It was a mistake to raise false hopes last night. I can't hire you. I don't trust you. Running a casino is hard enough. Sorry to have wasted your time."

She knitted her brows together, but never took her eyes from mine. "We didn't exactly get off on the best foot," she began.

"Doesn't matter," I cut in and reached for my wallet. "I'll reimburse you twenty bucks for showing up, but you really do need to leave and not come back."

The whiskey and wildflower scent of her power grew around me. She was setting a sound shield in place. "Now look here," I sputtered and summoned magic to thwart hers.

"Nay. You look here," she countered. "Hear me out—and this has nothing to do with a job. If you still want me to leave after I'm done, I shall."

I wasn't in a bargaining mood. That she still stood in my office was pissing me off. Yeah, she was a knockout, but Reno was full of showgirls. The reason this woman was so alluring was linked to her magic.

"Leave now." I pointed at the closed door. "And take your magic with you."

Her pleasant look departed; in its place, she bared her teeth and snarled. "The power you're so anxious to rid yourself of shields our conversation from curious ears."

Breath hissed from between my clenched teeth. "I know that. Who in the fuck would care what you have to say to me? Run back to your coven and—"

"There. Is. No. Coven. Look at me, Fae." She closed the distance between us. "Look damn good and close, and tell me what you see."

The temptation to raise power against her and toss

her out on her ear was strong, but so was my curiosity. What were another couple of minutes in the grand scheme of things? Deploying my talent, I probed her. Seconds later, my mouth gaped open. I shut it damned quick. How could I have missed something so elemental? She wasn't a Witch at all, but a forbidden fusion of Fae and Sidhe. Emphasis on forbidden.

"You missed the truth," she said sweetly, "because you saw what I wanted you to see. And yes, I forged a link to your mind to gauge your reaction. It's gone now."

"You did well to hide yourself from me," I growled. "I should shackle you and haul you back to Faery to face justice, but I'm fresh out of time. I will find you, though, and—"

"Oh really?" She arched her red brows. "I'm exceptionally good at concealing myself. Besides, just what would I be facing justice for? I'm not responsible for my parents' poor choices. What they did shaped my life, and not in good ways. You try being on the run for centuries with no place to call home."

"Fine. How about this?" I tried another tack since the court didn't need any additional matters to rule on with Faery teetering on the brink of disaster. "You walk out of here. I'll forget I ever saw you."

"It may come to that," she said. "The reason I'm here, in Lady Luck, is because Oberon tasked me with keeping tabs on you."

"What?" I shook my head, certain I hadn't heard right.

"I hire out my magical talents," she said, adding, "Now would be a good time to net me in a truth spell."

I unclamped my jaw, embarrassed to be reminded of such an elemental lapse. The woman nodded as the weave of my casting dropped over her. "Better. Oberon hired me. I'm just the most recent in a long line of spies who have kept eyes on you ever since he left Faery. Most of them didn't last long, and now I understand why."

I'd walked around my desk and perched on the edge, facing her. "Since I never knew I was being monitored," I said stiffly, "I fail to see how any action of mine would have impacted Oberon's..." I sputtered, at a loss for words. To call them spies made me so angry a red haze descended over my vision.

She waved me to silence. "Not you. Him. Last night, he sent a pack of mages to fire me. If I walked away quietly, he'd pay me half. If I persisted with my contracted activities, I'd get nothing." She blew out a tense breath. "I figure it's the same way he treated every-one. To avoid paying us for our services. I've been working this job for months and have yet to see so much as a dime."

"You must know where he is." The conclusion was so obvious, I should have jumped on it right away.

"That I do." She nodded. "Or more precisely, I know several possible locations. He moves around."

I narrowed my eyes. "Why are you telling me?"

A slight shrug. "I'm not certain. I could have vanished into the night. I'm good at that, but I'm sick of running. Beyond that, you got stuck being regent, and I figured you had a right to know Oberon's been playing hooky ever since he walked out on Faery."

Balancing my elbow on a knee, I rested my chin in my hand and regarded the Witch, who was really a Fae-Sidhe hybrid. "Ready to tell me your name?"

"Dariyah." She bowed formally and held out a hand. "Pleased to make your acquaintance Cynwrigg ap Llyr."

"And yours. It's not the name I use here, though. So you might want to call me Jed." I shook her hand, keeping the contact brief. A pleasant ripple of sensation shot up my arm from her touch. Hearing my true name, with all its trills, roll off her tongue in Gaelic was a delight and quite unexpected. No one had ever said my name on Earth before, not within the scope of my hearing. I understood why she'd built the sound shield now. Not because of my name but because of the information she'd imparted.

She licked her full lower lip. "After I left here last night, my temper got the better of me. Before I sent the Witch, wizard, and two shifters packing, I told them I was going to reveal everything to you."

"Probably not the smartest move. Where'd Oberon get mages to do his bidding?" I sputtered.

She shrugged again. "Same place he found me, probably. There's a central registry for wizardly types who do contract work."

First I'd heard of such a thing. "How does that work? Magic-wielders don't do well if they remain separated from Faery or the other magical realms for long."

"Most of us have ways of regenerating our talents. To answer your question about Oberon, maybe he's scrounging through worlds promising work and welching like he did to me." She closed her teeth over her lip. "I need to get over feeling sorry for myself, but I'm pissed. He not only stiffed me, he spied on me while I was spying for him."

"How?"

"He implanted a beacon in my cat that gave him a running tally of my activities."

My mouth twisted into a sour expression. I'd have at least tried to come up with something conciliatory to say, but what she'd described was vintage Oberon. He'd never been the trusting sort. I didn't see how Titania had stuck it out all those years with him, but I'd never looked too closely, either. They were my liege and his consort. What passed between them was none of my affair.

Dariyah clasped her hands in front of her. "I've said

what I came to say. I would still like to work with you, but I understand about trust. I've not given you any reason to view me as honorable, but I'd like to remedy that."

The corners of my mouth twitched; I spaded gobs of magic over my thoughts. I wanted her to be a whole lot of things that had nothing to do with honor. Clearing my throat, I said, "You don't really want to be a dealer or a waitress."

"No I don't, but both are good covers. Think about it. I seem to be out of work just now. We could team up. I could do other things that might help you." The Witch glamour clicked back into place, so opaque I couldn't drill through it. I was doing a bang-up job overlooking the obvious. Dariyah had a pile of power, so much I wasn't at all certain how mine would compare if we ever squared off against one another.

I narrowed my eyes and sent a speculative glance her way from beneath hooded lids. All the while, I deepened the sound shield she'd crafted, noticing my power slotted nicely with hers. It made sense. Fae magic was additive. "What exactly did you have in mind?"

"Working here." She frowned. "It's the topic of the hour, right?"

I shook my head. "Not what I meant. You suggested joining forces with me. What were you thinking we'd do?"

She doubled up a fist, but didn't punch the air. "Take that lofty Fae fucker down a peg or two."

"Won't work. Oberon is what he is. He'll never change." I blew out a breath. "Faery is in trouble. I need to cajole him into coming back. The land mourns his absence. She knows full well I'm not him."

Dariyah's frown deepened. "Faery is self-perpetuating. At least it's what Mother told me."

"Who was she?" I recognized my error immediately and followed my question with, "Never mind."

"I wouldn't have told you, anyway. Just so you don't waste your breath, I don't know who my father was. Back to Faery..."

I nodded. "The land has always taken care of its own needs. Until Oberon and Titania left. Then she became slovenly, slipshod. At some point along the way, a long narrow rift formed in her foundation. It's growing. The reason I opted for time on Earth was to attempt to locate it from this side. I can't do anything with it in Faery. No amount of magic makes a dent in the chasm's size or shape."

Dariyah snapped her fingers. "That's how I can help. I could search for it."

I started to say not without me, but held the words in check. If we located the rift from this side, I wouldn't need to deal with Oberon. Maybe. Assuming a generous blast of healing power set things right. The specter of sidestepping an unpleasant confrontation was damned appealing. I was plenty angry at him for abdicating his responsibilities to Faery. When I'd believed him missing, I'd been worried. Dariyah's information lent a whole different slant to everything.

"It's a good idea." I held up a hand. "On one condition. If you locate it, do nothing. You must give me your word you'll run straight back here and tell me where it is."

A corner of her full mouth twitched downward. "What are you afraid I might do?"

"Make it worse." Before she could protest, I kept my tone gentle when I said, "You have lived your life on borrowed time. We do not allow those like you to continue. Surely, you know that."

"Of course I know." She walked nearer to me, close enough I scented her annoyance. "Revealing myself to you was a huge gamble. You might have had henchmen here. I searched and only found your magic, but others could have been concealed."

"Go on," I urged.

"I loathe Oberon. I'll do anything to get back at him for what he did to me. He left you holding the shitty end of the stick too. Why aren't you more outraged?"

It was a reasonable question. Too bad I didn't have much in the way of answers. Telling her all of Faery made excuses for their liege made us sound like a bunch of saps.

When I didn't say anything, she went on. "Why do you want to find the breach first? Why not Oberon?"

"Because my problems with him will keep. The rift is growing worse. Presumably, Oberon knows about it, if he's been keeping an eye on everything." I gritted my teeth; it took effort to release my jaw to continue talking. The old fucker must know, and he'd done nothing. What the hell? Why was he moldering on the sidelines waiting for the land he ruled to implode? No wonder Faery had moaned so piteously.

"I see," Dariyah kept her tone even, noncommittal. Clearly, my priorities weren't meshing with hers.

"Back to the rift." I said. "It will recognize you for what you are and..."

"And what?" She shook her hair behind her shoulders.

"Honestly, I don't know what impact you would have. Maybe none. Maybe Faery would interpret your presence as one more nail in her coffin and rip herself to shreds."

Dariyah grimaced. "Nah. I'm not that important. But I will honor your request." She stuck out a hand. "I'm trying to build credibility, remember?"

I grasped her proffered hand and hung on to it. This time, a palpable shock ran from my fingers and along my arm. Her magic was more than powerful. It was amazing, and it was bleeding all over everything, including me.

"I will pay you, so keep track of the hours you work," I told her.

"Nope. I don't need money. What I said last night was a lie. But I welcome useful work. So much of what I do is smarmy. Spying on cheating husbands—and wives. Tracking down embezzlers. Booting escaped magical creatures who are creating havoc into Hell or Purgatory."

"It's an open offer." I was still holding on to her hand. The contact was muddling my brain and ramping up my body.

She took a step, then another, and tilted her head. Her lips were soft, inviting. Where her breasts pushed into my chest, I felt the stiff peaks of her nipples. My breath quickened, but I hesitated before lowering my mouth to hers. What harm could a kiss do? Just one kiss, and then she'd be on her way, and I'd make the rounds and ensure Lady Luck was ready to roll for one more night.

Her whiskey-and-wildflower scent enveloped me, and she threaded her arms around my back, holding me tight. My hands developed a mind of their own and settled over the luscious globes of her nice, tight ass. I tugged her against me and pressed my length against her stomach. My truth net frittered to nothing. I didn't need it. The weight of her mouth on mine was more potent than any spell.

Her mouth was sweet and alluring, and I licked the seam of her lips before thrusting my tongue inside. We stood like that for a long time, grappling with one another, trading kisses for sucks and bites. I felt her magic slam into my mind; the joining enhanced my arousal, twin to her own.

A staunch knock on my door put an end to my fantasies of turning her over and taking her spread-eagled across my desk. So much for my one-kiss promise. I dragged my mouth from hers long enough to yell, "Be out in a minute."

"We got a problem, boss," drifted through the door.

I shook my head. They always had problems, and a seeming inability to solve any of them without me. "We're out of time," I told Dariyah.

"It's all right." She smiled at me. "I've been out of time my whole life. See you later this evening. I'll hunt every night and check in before closing time." She unwound her arms and patted the bulge of my cock. "Hang on to that thought."

"Could get shut of it if I tried."

A sharp whiff of ozone presaged her departure. No portal, just a shimmery, glistening spot that winked out as she left. A downward glance told me I wasn't fit to do much of anything in my current state. I ducked into my small bathroom, shut the door, and freed my cock. A few hasty strokes were all it took before jism shot all over the tiny enclosure. Hasty strokes accompanied by graphic imagery of a naked Dariyah bouncing atop my erection.

Whoever was out there knocked again. With an exasperated sigh, I sent magic to clear away the mess I'd made, stuffed myself back into my trousers, and went out to face the world.

The crisis du jour was never as bad as they thought it was. I'd dispatch this one and go check on the room that had taken it up the shorts last night. In a few hours, Dariyah would return. Something to look forward to amidst my sea of unsolved problems.

CHAPTER FIVE, DARIYAH

I shouldn't have sashayed so close and tipped my head up in obvious invitation for Cyn to kiss me, but I couldn't help myself. He was tempting with a capital T, alluring as fuck, and I'd been dreaming about ways to seduce him for a long while. My body still tingled from being smushed against his, from the hot, hard length of him jammed into my stomach. I'd been choreographing ways to finesse a quickie when a knock on the door derailed my scheming.

Maybe when I returned early the following morning. I could coordinate things so it was nearly closing time, and— I pushed past my lust-ridden fantasies. They'd get in the way of a productive evening. My first stop was my flat. I wanted to check on Midnight, make certain he knew to run if he smelled anyone like me. I'd meant to do that before my trip to Lady Luck, but I'd been running late. The in-between place where I go to regenerate my power is captivating. I've always suspected if I stayed too long it would be hard to leave.

Mother had said Faery was like that. It got its claws into you until you were never genuinely happy anywhere else. She'd gone into exile to keep me safe, and lost a piece of her soul in the process. She never complained, but sometimes in unguarded moments when she wasn't aware I was watching her, she looked sad and defeated, shoulders slumped and the tiny lines around her eyes deeper than usual.

I'd asked why she couldn't go back to Faery without me, and she'd said because mages have long memories. No one had known for certain she was pregnant, but they'd cull through her mind if she returned. Besides, I had nothing to do with her crime, which had been falling for a Sidhe. The whole thing infuriated me. Mother was stuck in a magical grotto cut off from everyone while Father—whoever the hell he was—got off scot-free.

I'd mentioned that once, but Mother became so agitated, I never brought it up again. She'd said my father was a good man, not to judge him by circumstances. Pretty words, but it was impossible not to. When I was little, I'd nurtured secret daydreams about him coming to spirit me to Faery where there'd be a bit of finger-pointing and head-shaking. But in the end, the Fae and Sidhe and unicorns and everyone else welcomed me warmly.

Exile safely over, Mother rejoined Father, and we were a family cavorting through the lush greenery, majestic forests, and magical pools Mother had spun me tales of. Too bad none of it ever played out except in my head. My mother was still where she'd raised me, presumably. Father was in the wind, and I may as well be for all the freedom I'd had in my life.

Always skulking in shadows and glamouring up my true self to avoid detection had been a real barrel of laughs. If that weren't bad enough, like all those with Fae blood, I longed for Faery. Some nights it escalated to a physical ache that made me so miserable I almost couldn't function.

I always got over it, but I never moved beyond it happening again. And again. You'd think I'd be used to those episodes by now, except they'd done nothing but grow worse. In my more whimsical moments, I figured Faery was calling her errant daughter home to be slaughtered. That shaped me up damned fast.

The walls of my flat clicked into place around me, but I maintained a ward. Ready to flee at the first sign my home had been compromised, I was barely breathing as I sent tentacles of magic snaking outward. This would be my last visit here for a while.

Satisfied no one was lying in wait for me, I unraveled the shrouding protecting my unique energy signature and was rewarded with a startled yelp from Midnight. He bounded out from a corner he likes to hide in and jumped into my arms, digging his claws into me, and making little snuffling noises.

"You sound more like a baby piglet than a cat," I crooned and trolled lightly through his mind. Damn it. Something malevolent had set up shop right outside. Midnight been holed up for hours waiting for the source to leave.

Which meant it was still there. Fuck that crap. I'd show them a thing or two. A small shot of guilt reminded me I was supposed to be hunting for the breach beneath Faery. I get on it right after I was done here.

Keeping my mind voice soft and my magic muted, I told Midnight, *"Hide yourself. I will be back presently. The next time I leave, I'll bring you with me."* He didn't understand words, but concepts came through.

His compact, furry body pressed against me for a long moment. Not only wasn't he purring, he was trembling. The thing he'd labeled as evil had scared him, and very little did. Twenty-pound tomcats don't balk at much. I waited, offering him space to leave when he was ready. He nuzzled his snout into my neck and licked me with his sandpaper tongue. Seemingly understanding the need for stealth, he jumped down noiselessly and vanished into a different hidey-hole than the one he'd bolted from when I appeared.

I resurrected my warding and walked through a wall until I had a good view of the street. Naturally, I didn't see anything amiss. We magic-types are pros at hiding ourselves. Taking care to be as unobtrusive as possible, I sent a beam of seeking magic in a full circle.

Aha! There they were. Three mages. Didn't matter what they were. No one's magic is as strong as mine. Mother always said it was why those like me were anathema: because we could cut a path through anyone standing in our way. Anger simmered, very near the surface. Those dickwads had frightened my cat, and for what?

So long as I'd kicked the door to that topic open, how had Oberon turned my pet into a tracking device? I hoped he'd done it indirectly, and in a way Midnight never knew he'd been relegated to a minion of the Fae king.

Mortals strolled this way and that. The night was young. Quite young. It was the dinner hour for most folks. Because rents were cheap in this neighborhood, it was usually crowded with casino workers and others who supported Reno's brisk tourist trade. The congested streets and sidewalks would thin out, but not for a while.

I couldn't afford to wait that long. Oberon's thugs

were an appetizer. My real work would begin once I'd dispatched them. If I was Draconian enough about it, maybe he'd stop sending lackeys to make my life miserable, and... I rocked back on my heels. I'd met Oberon. Talked with him, signed a contract. Why didn't he know what I was?

I'd been well-coated in my Witch glamour, but surely the king of the Fae would be powerful enough to see through my disguise. Except he hadn't. Was that why he'd left Faery? Were his powers on the wane, and he needed to keep it a secret?

His magical connection to Faery might explain why the land was fading. Since they were linked, it would wither right along with him. Excitement thrummed through me. I felt certain I was onto something monumental.

Yeah, plenty monumental. Significant enough for Oberon to kill me himself once he found out I was privy to his secret. The thought brought a savage smile to my face. He might want to, but I seriously doubted he still had what it would take to end me. I'm tough to kill. All immortals are, but I'm more unyielding than most.

Whoa. My inner critic stepped up to the plate. *I don't know anything for certain. Not yet.*

She was right, of course. Rather than spinning my wheels in vengeful imaginings, I shifted my focus to the three mages hunkered a hundred yards away as they kept a close eye on the front door to my flat. What a bunch of dumb fucks. I might be teleporting inside. Or using the back door.

Following a hunch, I sidled to the other side of the building and checked to make certain more mages weren't stationed there. Nope. Just the three I'd sensed from within. Good. I didn't need any surprises. Edging back to my original position, I considered the humans littering the sidewalk. And all the cars. One of the first rules of magedom is not revealing ourselves to mortals. They suspect we exist, but we're more the purview of legends and fairytales.

I stifled a snort. Tinkerbelle was a far cry from the Kraken or a herd of rampaging Kelpies. Back in the day, humans understood faeries weren't all sweetness and light, but then along came Walt Disney, and all bets were off.

Faery's rules didn't exactly apply to me. It wasn't as if I were one of Oberon's subjects. Neither was I his hired hand any longer. So what if the children chatting up a storm with their parents got an eyeful—one that would give them nightmares for the rest of their lives?

Mmph. Even I'm not that much of a hard ass. What I settled on was risky because it would divert a portion of my power away from the fight, but it was the right things to do, and I'd make it work. It took me a moment to recreate the steps in the time-stopping spell. Once I had it, I chucked it over the street. Motion ground to a halt across a fifty-foot span of asphalt.

Not much I could do about folks on both sides of my casting. Even I don't carry enough magic to stop the world. However, my spell had one big bonus: my enemies were just as snared as the mortals. Sprinkling don't-look-here magic about like holy water—in case the mortals beyond the edges my enchantment turned into a bunch of looky-loos, I bounded to where I'd sensed the mages. Sure enough, a wizard, a shifter, and a Sidhe stood, mouths agape. They'd know exactly what was going on, but they were paralyzed.

Part of me—a miniscule part—cringed at how unfair the fight would be. Not a fight at all, but a rout. "I know you can hear me," I growled and slammed my fist into the wizard's face. Not the same dude as last night, but I bet they knew each other. His nose broke with a resounding crack. Blood sheeted down his mouth and chin. Reaching inside him, I clipped the moorings of his magical center, setting it free. A small cloud of golden feathery strands rose above him, effectively finishing him as a magic-wielder.

I'd be surprised if he could chase it down and reattach it. Without it, though, he'd just been busted back to mortal.

Next I turned to the Sidhe. A short blast of fire cut off one of his wings. He tried to howl, but couldn't open his mouth. A pathetic mewling was followed by strings of saliva. The pain was so intense, he wanted to puke, but couldn't.

"You're lucky number three," I told the shifter. "I'm not going to hurt you. Not this time. Go back to Oberon and tell him the next crew he sends against me —or my cat—will come back to him in body bags."

"Tell him yourself," a familiar voice ground out.

I spun to face the Fae King. Like I said, I've met him before. Tall and regal, he was garbed in a robe of gold and silver cloth embroidered with power words in the form of runes. Hair of spun silver was braided with hundreds of tiny jewels. He turned his patrician face with its high forehead, almond-shaped silver eyes, and thin, cruel mouth my way. The points of his ears had reddened with outrage.

"You heard what I had to say." I narrowed my eyes. "We're done. You hired me and fired me, and now you can leave me the fuck alone."

He shook his head, but his eerie gaze never left mine. "We will never be done. You declared war on me and mine when you chose to speak with Cynwrigg."

If I'd been smarter, I'd have teleported out of there. I had power to spare, even maintaining my glamour and my time-stopping spell. "You and yours?" I sneered. "That's rich. Don't sidestep your role in this by blaming me. Cyn had a right to know you were still alive and kicking. You declared war on him and all of Faery when you abandoned your people—your subjects—and your land to whatever fate might befall them. No ruler does that."

"How dare you judge me." Twin flames of fury reflected in the depths of his eyes, turning them molten.

"Not judging. Stating facts. Now if you'll excuse me, I have a long and busy night ahead of me. Just so we're clear, leave my cat alone. He's an innocent, one of the lives you used to be sworn to protect."

"I didn't hurt him."

"How do you know? You mucked around in his head. He might never be the same." I shook my head. "You're stalling. I'm not waiting around for the next batch of stooges to show up."

"Watch it, Witch. I command armies."

"You used to," I said oozing sweetness. "Last I checked, they report to Cynwrigg now."

Oberon's face darkened, bushy silver brows lowering like thunderclouds. Probably time to exit while the getting was good. He was trying to engage me, hold me in place for something. I had no desire to find out what. In one fell swoop, I dismantled my stop-time casting and leapt through an opening in the air.

I swooshed through my flat long enough to grab Midnight. "You're not going to like this," I told him before initiating another teleport spell. "Pretend it isn't happening."

Pathetic yowls accompanied us to the foothills of the mountains surrounding Reno as the cat did his damnedest to dig a hole in my arm and shoulder. Luckily, magic is superb for healing superficial injuries. My spell shattered around us. I was breathing hard, not so much from expended effort as from residual anger at Oberon.

What an overbearing prick he was. "Watch it, Witch," I mimicked in a singsong falsetto before stooping to set the cat on the ground. "Go hunt for mice," I told him. "I'll find you when I'm ready to go." Thoroughly freaked, the cat didn't wait for a second invitation. He ran as if Hellhounds were on his heels. He'd settle down once the adrenaline ran its course.

I walked to a nearby cliff and splayed my palms against it. Finding the breach had to be a matter of a process of elimination. I'd walk what I thought was one of many perimeters between Earth and Faery, checking every few feet. When I hit a spot that felt different, I'd explore it more deeply. Like as not, I'd locate the rift.

How hard could it be?

Don't get cocky. My resident critic was back. In this case, she was right. Cyn had been searching for quite some time with zero success. Presumably, he had more affinity for Faery than me. I cleared my mind of debris and my confrontation with Oberon and walked due north.

Every hundred yards or so, I stopped and sent magic auguring into the hillside. Hours passed with each test pinging back the same. I'd dismissed my glamour quite a while back to give myself access to the full spectrum of my power. Granted I'd expended quite a bit with my fancy-schmancy time spell, but it didn't take much to drill a hole and compare it to every other one I'd bored.

At some point, I felt Midnight running alongside me. There was a bounce to his step that hadn't been there before, and I was glad he'd gotten past the rude way I jerked him from what he believed was his home. We couldn't go back there. Hell, I'd be lucky to retrieve my few things without a magical horde breathing down my neck.

"First thing tomorrow," I promised Midnight, "I'll find us a new place to live, and I'll bury it so deep in spells no one will be able to find us." A glance at a crescent moon and the stars told me it was time to head back. I marked the spot I'd gotten to and loped back to where I'd begun, leaving a beacon there as well. No point in retracing steps I'd already taken.

Scooping up the cat, I whispered in its furry ears. "Once more, buddy. Sorry, but it's the quickest way." This time, I layered a calming spell around him. It seemed to do the trick because he was quiescent in my arms. Or maybe he was tired. Running on fight-or-flight chemicals takes it out of you.

I kept a shroud around us when I popped out a block or so from the casino. It turned out I needn't have bothered. The alley I'd selected was inhabited by sleeping drunks. Should I take the front door or teleport into Lady Luck?

Because I had kitty-man—and he was snoozing against me, all warm and purring—I opted for teleporting. My travel spells are usually spot on. This one was no exception. I shimmied through a wall at the far end of the upper floor. Cyn's office was only a few feet away. Still cautious, I kept my ward in place and scanned with magic, taking care to resurrect my glamour. Before I'd even peeked inside Cyn's office, the sound of raised voices told me someone else magical had arrived first.

Eavesdropping is one of the finest avenues to gather information. I heartily recommend it. Still concealed, I listened to a fellow who was presumably an emissary from Faery.

"You have to come home," he demanded.

"I can't," Cyn said. "For once, you'll have to handle things, Aedan."

"But the people—your people—are frantic. One of the unicorns gored another. It was an accident, but it freaked everyone out. When unicorns die, it means—"

"That the world is ending. Aye, I know that as well as

you." Cyn blew out a heavy breath before going on. "There's only one of me. If I leave here, I lose a cover I've established for myself, a reason to be here."

"Fuck that." Aedan's tone was shrill. "Be a bum. Why do you need a reason for anything? Oberon's balls! You're the prince of Faery."

"A dying land with a missing liege," Cyn said dryly. "Go home, Aedan. I'll be there as soon as I can."

"But the unicorn—"

"Draw everyone together. Hold a wake. That will give them something proactive to do."

"Got it." Aedan's tone made it clear he wasn't pleased.

I felt a blast of Fae power as he left and gave it about ten seconds before I knocked on Cyn's door.

Rather than relying on magic, he pulled it open and blinked as he stared up and down the hall muttering, "Now I'm hearing things?"

Before he could slam the door in my face, I dropped the ward I'd forgotten about. "Sorry. It's been a rough night."

He eyed me with Midnight in my arms. "Tell me you found something. I could use some good news." He stepped back and motioned me inside.

I shook my head and sketched out how my night had gone.

"You saw Oberon?"

"Yes. It didn't go well. I suspect his power is on the wane. It happens sometimes if the lore books are to be believed."

"Why would you think that?" Cynwrigg leaned forward, interest streaming from his blue eyes. Their real color was far more alluring, but I understood why dropping and resurrecting his glamour used more magic that leaving it in place.

"He has no idea I'm not a Witch. That's your first clue."

I'm not sure what I expected, but it wasn't the fierce smile that spread across Cyn's rugged features. "You may be onto something, Dariyah. When the club closes, we'll go hunting for him."

"I thought you were needed in Faery."

"Oh, you heard that?"

"I did."

He shrugged. "Eh. Aedan's more capable than he gives himself credit for. It will be good for him to handle this. Besides, it just means I'll be a little bit later, not that I won't show up at all."

Midnight twisted in my arms to stare at Cyn. After a moment, he resumed purring. "He likes you," I said.

"All animals do. It's a Fae thing. We have an affinity for them." He pointed to a seat. "Take a load off. Let me button up the club for the night, and then we'll be off."

"Best offer I've had all day." I sank onto a leather couch and kicked my feet up.

"There's food in the fridge. Help yourself. I'll be back soon."

"Thanks." Watching him leave, I marveled at how quickly we'd moved from an adversarial dancing around one another to functioning as a team. Or at least not taking one another's heads off.

"Nothing like a common enemy to forge alliances," I told the cat who meowed sagely as if he understood exactly what I meant. Moving him off my lap, I walked to the refrigerator and opened it intent on scrounging whatever was there. Who knew when my next meal would be?

Life on the run has taught me a whole lot of shit. Never turning down food or a place to pee were near the top of the list. Smiling at my own wit, I sat next to Midnight and proceeded to share cheese, tuna, and crackers with him. I hadn't given up on a tryst with Cyn, but it wasn't looking as likely as it had after the steamy kiss we'd shared. My nostrils twitched. The office smelled like him, and it inflamed all my senses.

"Mrowwww," was accompanied by a sharp nip.

Laughing, I filched another scrap of tuna and fed it to the cat.

CHAPTER SIX, CYN

I followed my usual pattern of checking on the club, starting with the basement and moving upward. The night had been uneventful; we'd made buckets of cash. Nothing quite like a casino to rake in the dough. A victim of mismanagement and embezzlement, this one had been teetering on the brink of ruin when I'd swooped in and picked it up for a song. Because I hid my acquisition behind a shell corporation, no one knew I owned the joint. They viewed me as the general manager, which was perfect.

It saved me from sorting through business propositions, none of which would have held the slightest interest. Organized crime is a happening thing in Nevada; they have their fingers in lots of pies. Casinos are a perpetual favorite because of the opportunities to blend under-the-table prostitution with games of chance. Both offer nearly endless possibilities for skimming off the top, bottom, and middle.

I didn't skim, but I paid part of my payroll in cash. Good, old invisible cash. Nothing quite like it. It saved everyone taxwise, including me. As I made the rounds, I parceled out twenties, fifties, and hundreds. The party line was it represented tips. Some of it actually did.

After telling everyone we'd have a general staff meeting at four the next afternoon, I hotfooted it back upstairs. Dariyah was waiting—and her cat. I was annoyed with Oberon for dragging the harmless creature into his perpetual schemes. What Aedan had imparted about the unicorns didn't bode well, either. Always a bit on the skittish side, they usually got along with each other.

How accidental had the goring been? According to Aedan, no one had actually seen it happen beyond the two unicorns involved. One was dead from a direct hit to her magical center. The other swore up and down it hadn't happened on purpose. She'd liked Rona, was devastated she was dead, and stood willing to make amends as needed.

There had to be more to it. Had they squabbled over a male? Over something else? I'd asked Aedan about other wounds. He'd said there weren't any, but unicorns heal so quickly if you're not actually looking at a laceration when it happens, you won't see a thing.

Eh, maybe I was making too much of a freak occurrence. Except it didn't feel that way. I've always had solid instincts, so I'd do well to heed my guts, and they screamed foul play. It appeared to be the way Dariyah functioned as well. How else would she have put a few unrelated bits together and come up with her theory about Oberon's power fading?

It was a brilliant deduction. Part of me hoped it was true, but a much bigger part didn't. Faery needed her liege. None of the rest of us who stood in line for the throne would do. Not at all. Oberon might be an ass, but he was our ass. I cringed at the thought and at all the times I should have stood up to him but had deferred.

At the time, I'd told myself it was to keep the peace, but my motivation had been far more self-serving. If I'd been too antagonistic, he'd have clipped the strands that bound me to the chain of succession. I'd seen it happen before. The dirty truth was it was how I'd moved to the head of the line. Back in the day, Titania had made a habit of challenging him. I didn't recall exactly when she'd faded from center stage, but I should have spoken up, taken her side since she was often right, and checked on her after she went missing.

As I considered it, I hadn't actually laid eyes on her for maybe fifty years. She'd bounced in and out of Faery after Oberon left, but her brief visits had ceased. Because they'd been so rare, I barely noticed their absence—until years had passed. Given my newfound information about Oberon, the change in Titania's pattern of dropping in worried me. Was she all right? I'd ask Aedan and those on the court I knew well, crafting subtle questions regarding her whereabouts. Anything more overt would add fuel to a pot that already threatened to boil over.

I pushed open the door to my office. Dariyah smiled up at me from her spot on the sofa. The cat had his snout in an empty tuna can. It rattled when he licked oil out of the bottom.

"Did you have enough to eat?" I asked. "I can always call down to the kitchen and have them send something hot up here."

"I'm fine," she replied and got to her feet. "Are you ready to leave?"

"Almost." Settling at the desk, I closed down the electronics, sealing them with encryption software. As I worked, I said, "I've been considering your theory about Oberon. It could explain why Faery is struggling."

"Exactly the conclusion I came up with." She nodded my way. "Mind if I ask a question?"

"Fire away."

"Mother said Oberon and Titania were linked to

both Faery and all its inhabitants. What happened to that after they left?"

I looked up. "One transferred to me, the other didn't."

"I'm guessing the one that didn't was the land itself." She arched a red brow.

"You'd have guessed right. When I started to sense the strands binding me to individuals and animals, I suspected I'd never see Oberon again. Couldn't figure out why the land didn't transition to me as well."

"Because Oberon never released it." She pursed her mouth into a tight line and went on. "He's nothing if not mobile. For all we know, he sneaks back into Faery and visits her behind everyone's backs."

I got to my feet. I had to stop making excuses for Oberon, whitewashing everything he did. "He's certainly capable of something along those lines," I agreed, disgusted with my level of restraint. If he was really doing that, it was horrendous because it hamstrung the land between the absent monarch and who she should be bonded with.

"Can you think of any other reason?" Dariyah persisted.

With her hands on her hips and her red hair swirling around her, she was a vision of loveliness. Nothing soft about her, though. Her beauty was tempered with an iron will. Guts and determination had carried her through what must have been a solitary existence offering scant emotional support.

"Not really," I replied. "Where do you think he might be?"

She scooped the cat into her arms. He growled, hackles raised, no doubt irritated at being separated from the tuna can. "It's a good question." She tilted her head to one side, brows drawn together in a thoughtful expression. "This might be playing dirty, but I say we return to my flat. He's bound to have posted spies after what I did to the three who were waiting for me earlier."

I grinned. "We grab one—or more—and convince them spying on you is a very bad idea."

"You've been reading my mail, honey." She stroked the cat to sooth him.

"What are you going to do with him?" I gestured at the cat.

"I'll set him free once I'm home. He's good at taking care of himself. I'm fairly certain he won't let anyone else get hold of him. When I stopped by my place earlier, he was apprehensive about the mages he sensed lurking outside. In his kitty mind, he saw them as dark and threatening."

"Good for him. He has solid instincts. Ready?" I locked my phone and tablet in my desk from long habit. Electronics didn't fare well in Faery. Something about the energy scrambled their innards.

Dariyah nodded. "At some point, hopefully tomorrow, I need to find another spot to call home. Midnight and I can't stay where we are."

"Would you like help?"

She narrowed her eyes my way. "Maybe. Thanks for the offer. I'm used to flying solo."

"I won't be overbearing. Promise. If you need assistance, let me know. Your problems are mostly my fault, and—"

"Bullcrap. I knew what I was getting into when I signed that contract with Oberon."

I'd been building a transport spell, but I stopped for two reasons. First off, I had no idea where she lived. But the second was she'd piqued my curiosity. "Why?"

"Why what?"

"Knowing you risked discovery, why'd you go to work for Oberon? Surely, there were other jobs through this central registry place."

Dariyah still cradled the cat against her. He'd settled in and crawled up her body until he was draped around her shoulders. "Faery exerts a pull. I'm far from immune to its power and magic. My Witch glamour is only a costume; it doesn't change who I am."

Her expression, resolute and sad, tore at me. Of course she'd long for Faery. It was mother to us all. Yearning for a land that would perpetually be closed to her must have shaped an indominable will.

"Do not say anything." She inserted spaces between the words. "I don't require your pity."

"I wasn't about to offer any." My tone was gruffer than I'd meant it to be. "I need to know where we're going."

"No you don't because I'll take us."

Power danced around her in visible bands of light that reminded me of an arcane kaleidoscope. My office vanished, replaced by a rather barren room permeated with her wonderful scents. Cinnamon, vanilla, and the sweet musk of her power. Midnight wriggled out of her arms and took off like a shot.

"He has his own routes in and out of here," Dariyah explained. "I've never located them, but then I never tried very hard, either."

"Maybe he has more magic that you give him credit for." Speaking of magic, I honed a strand and sent it zinging outward, searching for energies other than human.

"They're out there," Dariyah growled. "Exactly like I thought they'd be. Oberon's ego is too big to just walk away after I told him to go fuck himself."

I reeled in my casting. "I count three."

"Me too. Shall we? There shouldn't be much in our way this time of night. Earlier, I had to manage throngs of mortals and cars."

"How?" I angled a pointed look her way.

She shrugged. "A stop-time spell. It didn't cover a large enough area to truly conceal my actions, but it paralyzed the mages too, so I didn't have to keep it in place for very long."

I whistled. Her casual mention of magic that only the extremely powerful could command was a potent reminder of her skill.

"Eh. Don't offer up too much credit." Dariyah grinned and beckoned as we let ourselves out a small door off the kitchen.

I needed to monitor my thoughts since she was privy to most of them. I had no idea if it was a conscious effort on her part, or if her magic spilled over making certain she was well-informed about everyone in her immediate circle. Probably the latter. She'd been on her own forever and would have developed the habit of being vigilant.

We glided across an empty street, revealing ourselves at the last possible moment, and came face to face with three Fae. I swallowed shock. "You're supposed to be in the *Dreaming*," I sputtered, looking from one to the other. Two men and a woman, I remembered them well.

"We grew bored...Regent." A male with dark hair regarded me out of amber eyes. Garbed in U.S. trash-modern like the other two, he wore denim pants and a cotton shirt with snaps rather than buttons. Cowboy boots were the final touch; they made him fit right in in northern Nevada.

"Bored, huh?" I stopped there.

"You were wondering where Oberon got his underlings from. I guess that little puzzle's been solved." Dariyah spoke slowly, deliberately, taunting the Fae.

It was unusual—but not unheard of—for mages to leave the *Dreaming* after a long tenure there. A few of us bounced in and out as if it were a two-dollar whorehouse. Some checked in for a respite, never intending to remain, but this batch had been gone since maybe the 1700s. I dropped a truth net over the Fae. "What did he offer you?" I demanded, certain Oberon must have done something to sweeten the pie.

"A chance to make a difference." The woman tilted her chin at a defiant angle. Violet hair spilled around her shoulders.

"By subverting the natural order of Faery?" I stared at her and made a good-faith effort to hang on to my temper. It was a losing battle.

"You don't understand," the dark-haired man said.

"But you will," the woman chimed in.

I'd had enough of riddles and sanctimonious tidbits. I had a goddamned link to every other living creature in Faery. Last I checked, it was an all-or-none phenomenon. Rather like the land. Switching things up, I altered my truth casting and laced coercion into it.

"You will tell me where Oberon is." I gripped the man's upper arm plenty tight enough to hurt. He writhed in my grip and bared his teeth at me.

Something flickered at the corner of my eye. A wicked-looking serrated blade made of iridescent metal was gripped in Dariyah's hand. She pricked the point into the woman's neck.

"Let her go!" the other man shouted and jumped at Dariyah. Jumped and splatted against a barrier that sent him flying backward through the air, silver hair swishing every which way.

"Nice try." Dariyah exerted pressure on the blade until a trickle of blood ran down the woman's neck. I'd been trying to remember her name, but it escaped me. Like the other two, she'd abandoned Faery for the *Dreaming* centuries before. Immortality dragged on many, made it impossible for them to keep on keeping on. She'd traded one immortal life for another far sooner than most, which made me intensely curious just what inducements Oberon had come up with.

Searing pain shot up my arm. The fellow I was hanging on to had sunk his teeth into my wrist. I punched him in the face, gratified to hear the *thwack* of bones breaking in his cheeks. Following up on my advantage, I drove him to the ground and straddled him.

"Where is Oberon? What did you mean about making a difference?" I punched him again. Blood gushed from his nose, but I felt him summon healing threads to put himself back together. I reached for the spot I should be linked to him—not there. Trying again in a different location, I came up with the same result.

How had Oberon managed the impossible? Somehow he'd separated some of Faery's residents from my hold on them.

"Got it," Dariyah crowed. "Let's go."

"Got what?" The woman with blood sheeting down her neck sounded dazed.

"The information we need." Dariyah released the hold she'd had on the Fae—a magical one because she hadn't been touching her. The Fae crumpled to the ground and rolled to her knees, never taking her gaze from Dariyah.

"Pah. You have nothing," she retorted. "Witches can't read minds."

"This one can." Dariyah offered a saccharine smile.

The Fae who'd ended up on his ass raced forward and cradled the kneeling female in his arms. "Are you all right?"

"Of course. Stop fussing over me." Batting him away, she got her feet under her and stood.

"You will talk," I growled at the Fae trapped between my legs. "If you do not, I will hunt you down in the *Dreaming* and drag you before the court to face justice."

"I've done naught wrong," he protested, his words thick and slurred.

"That's for the court to determine."

"Pfft. A bunch of misfits. We are the beginnings of a new race, a pure one," he informed me.

"Shut up!" the woman squealed.

I'd heard enough. Oberon had planted plenty of seeds about establishing a magical master race, one unsullied by any other type of magic-wielder. He'd always thought Faery should be limited to Fae, and all its other inhabitants booted out to fend for themselves.

"We need to go," Dariyah said.

I jumped upright and motioned her close while eying the Fae who'd all drawn near one another. The other two had dragged the one I'd injured to his feet. "You will remain here for the next hour," I informed them.

"We don't report to you," the silver-haired man said.

"In this instance, you do," I told him and dropped the casting I'd been working on over all three of them. It clicked into place, staves thickening as they set up.

Dariyah ran her hands over my impromptu prison, strengthening my efforts. "Won't hold them forever," she said, "but we don't require forever."

"What are you?" the woman demanded.

"She can't be a Witch," the Fae with the ruined face mumbled.

"You've grown soft and weak," Dariyah mocked

them. "So out of practice from lolling around in the *Dreaming* you've forgotten what real power looks like."

A cloud scented with herbs and wildflowers descended as she swept us into a travel spell. "Do you really know where Oberon is?" I asked.

"I know where he was when we left," she replied. "He maintains a network for his minions so they can always find him if they have to. Besides, I'm familiar with many of his usual haunts."

I'd been inside the one Fae's mind. How had I missed the network? I set my mouth in a tense line. "Him poaching from the *Dreaming* is disturbing."

"Yeah, it's not good at all," Dariyah agreed. "We may have clipped their wings in terms of teleporting, but they can ping Oberon through the same ingenious mechanism that allowed me to pin down a location for him. Hang on, almost there."

"He won't be," I said dully.

"You can't know that."

"Aye, I can and do. He's not ready to face me, or I'd already have gone rounds with him."

The splash of water over rocks was accompanied by rich pine smells as a forest shaped up around us. My nostrils twitched. Oberon had been in this spot, and not very long ago. True to my prediction, though, the place was deserted. A smoldering fire in the middle of a small rock circle was the only indication anyone had been here recently.

"What was that master magical race crap?" Dariyah paced in a tight circle, clearly irritated our prey had flown the coop.

Not surprised by Oberon's abrupt departure, I turned to her. "He believes Faery should only succor the Fae, but our compact with the land includes all varieties of magic wielders. Not that we've ever had many shifters or Witches other than passing through, but we've always provided a home for any mage wishing to settle there."

"So he grew tired of waiting for a perfect world?" Dariyah angled her head to one side.

"Maybe so."

"Any idea what his strategy is?" she asked.

"Aye. He's letting Faery implode, so he can begin anew and craft the kind of realm he's always wanted. The land must know. It has to be why she's pitching fits."

"We have to stop him."

The sight of her features, rigid with determination, touched me. I dropped my hands onto her shoulders. "Quite a display of loyalty to a land you've never seen, one that forced you into exile."

She shrugged out from under my grasp. "It's hard to miss something I've never had, but I do know right from wrong. We cannot let him get away with subverting

Faery, making it into something it was never meant to be."

Her words had a sobering effect, reminding me the land might rebel, casting all of Oberon's careful planning asunder. Now that I knew more, it would be worth trying to talk with her again.

Dariyah had perched on a flat rock and was leaning toward the dregs of the fire, hands extended to catch its residual warmth. "What do you want to do next?"

I sank to a crouch next to her. "I have to return to Faery."

"That's right," She nodded. "I'd forgotten about the unicorns. Well then, I'll do more hunting for the rift, and we can talk tomorrow after I've staked out a new place to live."

I didn't plan my next words; they popped out on their own. "Would you like to accompany me?" I asked, keeping my tone formal.

She swiveled to face me, eagerness spilling from her green eyes. "Hell yeah, I would, but doesn't it break a bunch of rules? I can hide what I am from whomever we run into, but the land will know I don't belong there."

I met her forthright gaze. "You deserve time in Faery as much as anyone else with Fae blood. Or Sidhe blood for that matter. I've had time to think about it, and I'm appalled at our archaic rules that have kept you out. As you mentioned, you're scarcely responsible for your parents' poor choices."

"There's more," she prodded, and I remembered her proclivity for living in my mind.

I stood and drew her to her feet, circling my arms around her. "There is, indeed. I don't want to be separated from you. Not quite yet." Maybe not ever, but I wasn't ready to give voice to that part. We might be working together, but our alliance was fragile. She'd been on the run all her life and probably valued freedom above all else.

"We should go," she murmured.

"We will." I smiled down at her and crushed my mouth over hers because I couldn't resist the temptation of her full lips a moment longer.

❧ 7 ❧

CHAPTER SEVEN, DARIYAH

I'd hoped we'd be quick enough to catch Oberon. We hadn't been. Not that I wanted to go another round with him, but Cyn deserved a chance to challenge the Fae king. Could he force him to back down? I had no idea. I didn't know much about the actual structure of Faery other than that it was ruled by a court. Whether every representative had an equal voice, or whether they could be overruled in the blink of an eye was an unknown.

Somehow I couldn't see Oberon agreeing to anything he didn't support merely because a preponderance of his subjects wanted things to roll that way. When I'd quizzed Mother about Faery, she generally demurred. It made sense since the land was barred to me. Or so we'd thought. I'd planned on spending what was left of the night hunting for a way to access the rift, but that was before Cyn invited me to Faery.

I still couldn't quite believe he'd done that. Neither could I believe I was cradled in his arms kissing him. The last time had been a spontaneous gesture on my part. Because he cut such a stunning figure, I'd given in to the heat and need and hunger crackling through me like an out-of-control bonfire. The same desperate craving filled me now, sparking from our smushed-together mouths to every cell in my body.

I arched into him, my back bending like a bow as I sought to eradicate every stray air molecule separating us. The closer I got, the more intense the feel of acres of muscles pressing against me. My nipples peaked with lust, and I straddled one of his legs, forcing the core of me against his thigh. All the moisture in my body headed south; my sex slicked with desire. Cyn's arms tightened around me, and he lashed his tongue back and forth, painting the inside of my mouth. I sparred with him until we traded as he welcomed my probing tongue. His lips were firm, a sensory joy when he changed up our kiss from bites to sucks to nibbles to tongue-action, and then back again in an endless circle of delight.

Moaning and rocking against him, I gave in to sensation crashing through me. His hands gripped my ass, and his cock radiated heat, its hardness pressing into my belly. I wanted that cock with a singlemindedness that shocked me. No stranger to sex, it had always been more of a wham-bam-thank-you-now-go-away proposition. Not the lush, magical event unfolding around me.

I'd twisted the fabric of his shirt in my hands as I grappled with getting him as close as I could. In the distant recesses of my mind, I knew we should get moving. We both had things to do, and if this pony got any farther down the track, we'd be here for hours.

Even knowing that, I snaked a hand between us and curved it around his cock. Long, thick, and harder than hard, its proportions tantalized me. I imagined how it would stretch me, plumb me. Awash in sensual imagery of him on top of me, behind me, beneath me, in my mouth, I rocked faster, stoking my lust on his thigh. He made a low, guttural, very male sound that reminded me of a lion stalking his mate. I loved that noise. It made me hotter than hell.

He jammed a hand into the junction between my legs, fingers rubbing me through my pants. I wanted him with a singlemindedness that blinded me, but not like this. We deserved a bed. I wanted to see him naked, not rely on my imagination to guess what he looked like. I was panting, heart beating so hard it wanted to jump out of my chest. The answering throb of his pulse danced beneath my mouth as I strung kisses up and down his neck.

Lifting my mouth from his flesh was one of the

hardest things I've ever done. I moved my hand from his cock and placed it over the one between my legs to still his busy fingers. "Not like this," I rasped, amazed I could match thoughts to words.

He focused his gorgeous gold-and-silver eyes with their rich copper centers on me. "Anything you want, darling. Just tell me."

Nodding, I swallowed around a throat that had gone dry with desire. "We, you and me, have important tasks to accomplish. I want you. Damn, but I want you. If we remain here, though, we won't leave for hours."

Cyn touched the corner of my mouth with a finger. "Ah, the voice of reason. You're right, of course, but you're delectable, tantalizing." He cupped the side of my face. "Not much diverts me from duty. You've accomplished the impossible."

I felt my face warm; the compliment pleased me. I hadn't been the recipient of very many of them. "Can I sign up for a rain check?" My nether regions tingled; I ached to leap back into his arms.

He nodded. "Lots of rain checks."

"I'll hold you to it. Fae promises are binding."

"If I ever meet that mother of yours, I'll make sure she knows she taught you the important things."

The time in his arms had blasted through my usual barriers, leaving me far less guarded than normal. When he mentioned Mother, it reminded me how much I missed her, and I blinked back tears. I turned away, but he was only inches from me. Even if he'd been on the far side of the fire pit, I had a feeling not much escaped him.

He turned my face toward him again and traced the track of a tear down one cheek. "Did I say something wrong?"

I shook my head. "Not at all. I miss her. It's been a long, long time since we parted ways. She made me promise it would be forever when I left. I understood why we couldn't see each other, but I never truly accepted it. If I made a bunch of trips back and forth, all of which would require a hefty output of magic, someone would have noticed sooner or later. And then she'd have to run again."

He'd glued a thousand percent of his focus directly on me. It felt both discomforting and welcome, wrapped up in a bewildering mélange of confusion. No one had paid me any heed since I left the small world Mother and I called home. Nor had I wanted them to. The less attention turned my way, the less I had to worry someone would catch a glimpse beneath my glamour.

"The place you settled, was it difficult to find?" he asked.

"Very. I was five when we finally quit scuttling from place to place."

He traced the line of my cheekbone with a thumb. "She must have loved you very much."

"What an odd thing to say. Of course, she did. She was my mother."

Cyn shook his head. "She is far from the first woman faced with the prospect of a mixed breed child. Nearly all of them make a different choice."

Hearing him say that was unnerving. I'd assumed many magical women sought refuge away from Faery—or other magical worlds—to rear their hybrid babies.

"What is it?" His hand still curved around the side of my face, and he smoothed locks of hair out of the way.

"I don't know. Nothing. Everything. I get the part about feeling an immediate alteration when life begins within you. It never occurred to me anyone would..." Finding words became a struggle.

"The price for such a child is death." Cyn's voice was gentle but his message wasn't. "Permanent death, not banishment to the *Dreaming*. Your mother was courageous, dedicated to living life on her own terms."

A corner of my mouth twitched into half a smile. "That's Mom all right. I sometimes prayed to the goddess to gift me with half of her strength."

"I'd say your wishes were heard."

A surge of power wafted near us, the whiskey and wildflower scent heady. Cyn wrapped both arms firmly around me, holding me next to him as his travel spell swept us away. I'd meant to explore a little to see exactly where we'd been. I could still do that, but I suspected it was the hinterlands in northern Nevada or maybe southern Oregon.

"I'll bring us out in my rooms in Dubrova Castle," Cyn said. "It will give you a private place to make certain your disguise is well in place. And it will provide an opportunity to absorb your first taste of Faery. It's overwhelming after time on Earth."

"Overwhelming, how?"

"Everything is more intense. Tastes. Smells. Colors are sharper. Emotions more concentrated. The newness of it all will wear off quickly, but it's best if your initial moments aren't marred by curious passersby who want to know all about you."

"I guess they'd know I wasn't from Faery, huh?"

Cyn chuckled. "Aye, they'd know, right enough. The land puts her mark on everyone there."

My excitement crumpled. "But not me. She'll never include me."

He stroked my back with gentle hands, rubbing tension away. "I don't know. Times are changing, perhaps rather radically. Let's take this a step at a time."

"Won't be hard to do. Up until a short while ago, I'd written off Faery. I'll be satisfied by a visit, no matter how brief it is, because I never expected to get even that much."

I felt the transition point in his spell when we passed from Earth into Faery. Felt is a massive understatement. A barrage of what I can only label as belongingness slammed into me. A sense of rightness, of finally being where I'd been born to be began in my toes and raced through me like high voltage energy. Moments later, a large room took shape around us. Set into a corner of the building, it had banks of leaded-glass windows on two sides. Muted light streamed through, illuminating a quietly understated masculine environment.

The space was neat. Nothing strewn on the bed or floor, which suggested Cyn put his toys away. And his clothing. Or maybe he had servants to cater to his every need. The concept was so foreign to me, I shoved it aside.

A massive four-poster bed with richly carved head and footboards sat against a wall facing the windows. It was covered with expensive-looking fur throws that had to be real. Where would someone come up with plastic or polyester in a place like Faery? Dressers and armoires crafted from matching wood were scattered about. A desk was tucked into the windowed corner, but I didn't see a computer monitor. Maybe he got by with a laptop. A door at one end suggested either a closet or a bathroom, and every free bit of wall space was lined with overly full bookshelves.

"Do my quarters pass inspection?" Cyn's question held soft humor.

My cheeks grew warm. "I wasn't meaning to come off as a house monitor," I murmured. "It's a lovely room, cozy and habitable. Where is your computer?"

"No Wi-Fi in Faery. Nothing electronic here. The chips or whatever they're made with don't play nicely with this much magic."

Interesting. I hadn't known. Meanwhile, the overwhelming sense of coming home had done nothing but grow stronger. I wished I could let Mother know I'd finally crossed into Faery, but recognized it for foolishness. She'd view what I was doing as a totally avoidable risk. I could see her shaking a finger in my face and telling me I was an idiot.

Mages here would see her blood within me, and then her ugly secret would be out. If she didn't already have a price on her head, she would once people got a gander at me. I swallowed hard, determined to remain deeply hidden. This side trip had been nothing but sheer indulgence on my part. I'd be damned if my stupidity came back to bite Mother.

"Would you like something to drink?" Cyn asked.

"Sure. Maybe just water."

He crossed the room and pushed the door open. When he emerged, he carried a cut-crystal decanter filled to the brim with water. So I'd been right about the door leading to a bathroom. Taking the glass from him, I drank and drank. I'd known I was thirsty, but not how thirsty.

A sense of peace like nothing I'd ever known before sank into my bones. I closed my eyes for a moment and sighed with pleasure. When I opened them, I said, "You don't need to babysit me. They're probably waiting for you somewhere."

"Everyone is downstairs in the courtyard holding a wake for the unicorn."

Guilt pricked. "Please. Don't let me hold you up."

He extended a hand, but I shook my head. "No. This is between you and your people. I don't want to dilute anyone's mourning with curiosity as they wonder who the fuck I am."

"All right. I'll return for you presently. Don't leave without me."

"How about if I ward myself?"

"No such thing as a ward people can't see through in Faery. This isn't anything like Earth where you can conceal yourself in perpetuity if you don't want to be noticed."

"I'll behave. Promise. You run along." I made shooing motions. The sooner he dealt with the unicorn problem, the sooner we could get back to the real work, which was locating the breach. I didn't let myself think about being alone with him, or the bedroom that carried his delightful scent. Maybe later, after we'd figured a few things out, we could steal a few moments to ourselves. Until then we couldn't afford to waste any time.

I felt the bite of his magic as he probed deep, maybe seeing if I was being truthful. He waved a hand and a platter of cut up cheese and bread materialized. "Help yourself. I'll return as soon as I can." He cocked his head to one side, eyeing me intently.

"Is everything all right?" Worry ate at me that maybe he'd seen something, and I couldn't remain after all.

He nodded. "More than all right. Faery has marked you as hers."

Had that been the cascade of rightness I'd sensed. "But how?" I stammered.

"How does anything happen here? Back soon."

I expected him to walk out the door; instead he vanished. One minute he was there smiling at me, the next he was gone. I could still smell his unique scent, feel his energy signature, but he'd left. Rather like with the water, I hadn't realized how hungry I was until I started layering cheese slices on fresh-baked bread and eating them as quickly as they were assembled. Soon, only the platter remained. It was crafted of bone china so fine it was nearly translucent, and I picked it up, marveling at the workmanship.

Was everything in Faery a class act? It certainly appeared so. Maybe there were ghetto areas where the less fortunate congregated, but I doubted it. Not much that magic couldn't fix or buy or change. And everyone in Faery boasted some type of power.

Walking to the windows, I looked out at lush vegetation. It stretched in all directions outside the wall that circled the castle. What had Cyn called it? Dubrova. That was it. Did the name have a special meaning? I tugged on a sash, and one of the windows swung outward. I inhaled deeply. Faery smelled like green growing things and a restless sea mixed into one. The effect was fresh, pure, invigorating. There was at least one ocean here and several lakes, streams, and pools. Mother had told me about them before she decided talking about Faery wasn't the best idea. Why build desire for a place I could never visit?

I itched to wander about, but I'd given my word. The high, sweet notes of a flute caught my attention. Below me, a procession of nymphs, satyrs, Fae, Sidhe, and unicorns walked in a solemn line followed by many smaller animals. Birds circled overhead: hawks and owls and songbirds. Toward the end of the procession, four unicorns carted a bier suspended from their necks by golden cords. The dead unicorn had been lashed to it.

I couldn't help myself. I reached out with magic, determined to read the last of the creature's thoughts before it succumbed. Enough angst scoured the crowd, I didn't believe anyone would notice my actions. One of the pallbearers neighed and stamped his feet. The others shushed him. I whipped my head inside, but didn't shut the window. I was still connected to the corpse, searching for clues that might help Cynwrigg.

He'd offered me a boon with this unexpected jaunt into Faery. I'm all about paying my debts, and maybe I'd come up with something useful. I cringed as the unicorn's last moments played out before me. I was leaning out the window again to make certain I didn't miss anything. She'd been walking along, minding her business and thinking about a particularly rich patch of pasture she'd been saving for herself when the other unicorn had trotted up beside her. She'd been glad to see Soir, and they'd chatted of this and that. Something dark and opaque settled over them, forcing them to halt. Rona, the dead one, had panicked. Soir dropped into some kind of trance. Slowly, deliberately, she'd turned and driven her horn into Rona. Because she hadn't taken time to probe, I assumed whoever was calling the shots controlled her strike.

Once Rona was on the ground, lifeblood draining onto the ground, the curtain had lifted. Soir wore such a shocked look, I felt sorry for her. Falling to her knees, she'd settled magic around Rona and tried to halt the hemorrhaging. If Rona's magic had been intact, she'd probably still be alive, but I saw it float away in a golden ball while Soir bent over her, long neck curved in determination and hoofs splayed over her friend's inert form. When she understood all was lost, she'd bugled madly, neighing and stamping until creatures streamed out of the thick foliage to investigate.

I shifted focus, backpedaled, and attempted to track the source of the insidious casting that had snared the unicorns. No luck. Curling one hand into a fist, I punched the air and dismantled my spell. Goddess be damned. Evil walked in Faery. Where would it strike next? More pertinently, how come no one else had thought to pull her last thoughts from the dead unicorn?

Rona's body had been placed within a circle of wooden staves. Far below me, Cyn and Aedan chanted, consigning her to cleansing magefire. It crackled around the unicorn, driven by the magic that had spawned it and burning with a mind of its own. If the words Cyn chanted were true, Rona would live on forever in a Valhalla-like place, or rather her spirit would.

Her death saddened me. It had been the work of someone truly evil. They'd have to reside within Faery's boundaries to ply their maliciousness. It was horrendous news to tell Cynwrigg, but I had no choice. If he knew, he could scour far and wide and root out whatever wished to sow discontent in this enchanted place.

My money was on Oberon. I drew back and pulled the window into place, latching it. Where was Titania? Mother had always spoken of them as a unit, but my contract had only been with him. More pertinently—since perhaps she didn't dirty her hands with business matters—Cyn never mentioned her. Had she retired to the *Dreaming*? Mouthed off one too many times and been banished?

If I got a vote, it would be for something like the latter.

The group ranged around the bier were singing now. Something in a minor key in Gaelic that made my heart hurt. Cyn had said emotions were rawer here, closer to the surface. I'd just downed another glass of water I'd fetched from a bathroom done up in white marble, when someone knocked on Cyn's door.

It couldn't be him. He'd just walk through a wall or something. Even if my ward wouldn't be much of a deterrent, I built a hasty one and ducked into the largest of the armoires. It was a tight fit with rows of pants and jackets at staggered heights, but I wouldn't have to be in here long, either.

I hoped.

Sure enough, the knob turned and the door to Cynwrigg's rooms creaked open. "Come out, come out wherever you are," a high-pitched voice invited.

Like fuck I will.

I couldn't see through the thick cherrywood of the armoire, but my magical senses are well-honed, so I relied on them in conjunction with my ears and nose.

My unexpected visitor was Fae and male and quite mad since he kept on chanting that single line from a children's game.

Heavy footsteps were accompanied by the distinctive feel of Cyn's energy. "What are you doing in my rooms, Ysir?"

"Someone broke in, Regent. Yes, they did. I felt them. I smelled them. Fee, fi, foe, fum, I smell the—"

"Enough. Leave now."

"But, Regent—"

"We're all on edge today. Return to your library, Ysir. Do it now."

Even buried in the armoire I felt the blast of coercion that went along with Cyn's orders.

"Aye, my lord. Right away my lord." Footsteps pattered down a hall I'd never seen. The heavy door slammed shut, and I exited the wardrobe as quietly as I could manage.

"Who in the hell—" I began, but Cyn lifted a finger to his mouth. Yeah. Good advice. I switched to telepathy, although magic is sometimes easier to sense than words are to hear. *"Who was that?"*

"The librarian. He's been...off for many, many years, but there's nothing wrong with his magic. Still, I don't understand how he picked up on your presence here."

I crossed the room to where Cyn stood. *"There's something I have to tell you."*

"Can it wait? I only returned because I sensed Ysir was here."

I shook my head. *"No. It can't. It might be the lynchpin that brings everything into focus."* Without stopping, I launched into what I'd dredged out of the dead unicorn's mind.

❧ 8 ❧

CHAPTER EIGHT, CYN

I listened to Dariyah with a spreading sense of horror as we stood toe-to-toe with one another. Who would target unicorns? The most whimsical of magical creatures, they were loved and valued by all. Which was precisely why they'd been chosen. To make a point. And a vicious one at that. And then there was the legend about unicorn deaths portending the end of Faery.

"Cyn?" Dariyah's green eyes bored into me.

Strategies flashed through my mind, each of them imperfect and discarded almost as soon as they appeared. I pinched the bridge of my nose to encourage rational thought. I was outraged, wound too tightly to make anything akin to a logical decision.

"Has anything like this happened before?" Dariyah asked. She'd shelved telepathy, but Ysir was long gone.

"Nay. Never." I reverted to Gaelic, a sure indicator of my mental turmoil.

"You must have enemies," she persisted.

I shook my head. "Dragons are our allies. A strike against us is the same as a strike against them. No one has ever been willing to alienate them. The consequences for such an act would be disastrous."

Her eyebrows shot up. "Dragons, eh? I'd love to meet one, but it's beside the point." She raked a hand through her thick curls. "It appears you have a brand-new problem."

"Pfft. Would that it were only one." I held up a hand, counting off on my fingers. "Oberon is on the rampage, determined to recraft Faery in his image of a Fae-only realm. The land is crying out for help, perhaps slowly dying. Or not so slowly. And now you tell me darkness has violated our borders and is wreaking havoc."

"They're all related. They'd almost have to be. I don't believe in coincidental catastrophes." Dariyah closed her teeth over her lower lip and bit hard enough to leave small impressions.

"No doubt." My jaws were clenched. I relaxed them so my next words wouldn't come out garbled. "I need to call an emergency session of our court. It will provide an opportunity for everyone to weigh in."

I must have scoured her with a speculative glance because she frowned. "What? Have I suddenly grown a second head?"

I raised a hand in front of me, changed my mind, and touched one of hers. "Nothing like that. I'm figuring out what has to happen next. I can't bring you to court. I can't leave you here. If something about your magical emanations caught Ysir's attention, it could easily happen again. Perhaps not with him, but with another of Faery's residents."

"I understand. I was planning to leave soon anyway." In contrast to her words, her shoulders slumped, and she looked away.

I placed a finger beneath her chin, tilting it until she met my gaze again. "Understanding something and accepting it are not the same. I'm sorry. I'd like nothing better than for circumstances to be different."

She nodded once. "I get it. You have to provide leadership. If anyone figures out what I am, that you broke a cardinal rule by bringing me to Faery for anything other than my funeral, their confidence in you will be called into question."

Her insight was so accurate, it fascinated me. I should have hightailed it back to the courtyard. Instead, I gathered her close and held her against me. "Do you have to be so damned noble? Can't you beat your breast and scream it's not fair?"

She threaded her arms around me. "What good would it do? I've had my moments—lots of them—when I hated everyone who walked beneath Faery's skies. Resented both Fae and Sidhe who'd dumped me into an untenable position. And then I pulled my head out of my ass and stopped feeling sorry for myself. Besides, my presence here puts Mother at risk. If anyone figures out what I am, they'll see her blood within me."

Raucous bugling snapped my head around.

"Dragons! Those are dragons." Dariyah wriggled out of my embrace and ran to a window. By the time she got there, all I felt was energy. She'd cloaked herself, becoming invisible. Smart of her. Dragons don't miss much.

I joined her half expecting to see an entire flight of wyrms darkening Faery's skies. It would mean Fire Mountain's volcanoes had upped the ante, and the dragons' world had vanished beneath a flood of molten rocks. Breath rattled from my lungs when I only counted three. Someone was looking out for me. I did not want an influx of close to a hundred dragons on top of everything else.

"Oooohhhhh, they're magnificent," Dariyah crooned. "Simply incredible. What a treat."

I made an effort to see them through her eyes. To mine, they were problem number four. I'd forgotten about them when I was listing all the difficulties facing us. "They're here for a reason," I cautioned her. "Their world is experiencing its own set of troubles."

She stepped away from the windows and dropped her ward. "They live in a place called Fire Mountain, right?"

"Aye. They do. It's a hot, barren place. All rocks and sand with twin suns that put out an ungodly amount of heat, but the dragons adore it. The land is ringed with volcanoes. Last time they showed up here, it was to warn us."

"About?" Dariyah craned her neck to sneak another peek at the dragons. Below window level, they were circling to land.

"Several of the volcanoes were erupting. They feared it would become universal, and their world would be destroyed. If that occurred, they planned to relocate here, but I suggested they hunt for a place better suited to their needs."

"It can't be coincidental." She repeated her earlier skepticism.

"What do you mean?" I asked.

She drew herself up straighter after a final glance outside. "Your problems here and their problems there must be linked somehow."

"Aye. I thought much the same since our lands are connected. One more issue to toss before the court.

Many minds often perceive what a single one misses. See you back on Earth."

"Yes. You will. I'll attempt to make progress locating the rift, and I need to find another apartment." She smiled. "No worries. I have plenty to do today."

I didn't want her to leave. It was irrational and downright dangerous. What she'd said about my subjects losing faith in me if her presence were discovered was spot on. I'd never given a second thought to how arbitrary some of our laws were, but now wasn't the time to start picking them apart.

She moved close to me, rose on tiptoe, and kissed me once, urgent and sweet, before twirling out of reach. Mid-twirl, she vanished through a space in the air that sewed itself shut behind her. It was an elegant move, one designed for subtlety and to cover all traces of her presence in my rooms.

More bugling lit a fire under me. I dashed through the door and ran briskly down several flights of stairs and a long corridor leading to a side door into the courtyard. I didn't ever pay much attention to Dubrova castle, but it's a grand place decorated with priceless art in all forms: wall-hangings, sculptures, figurines, crystals, charms, paintings, cunningly woven carpets. Made of glass and stone and wood and magic, the castle changed from day to day. Sometimes corridors no longer led where I expected them to.

Today, my path was direct. Perhaps the structure sensed my need for haste. Maybe it had detected Dariyah's presence and alerted Ysir. Something had. The ancient librarian was usually buried in dusty tomes and scrolls. On a good day, he remembered who I was, but usually he mistook me for Oberon.

The unicorn had been reduced to a heap of glowing ashes. Everyone was still singing or chanting our dirge for the departed. The dragons, a different batch than the ones who'd arrived last time, stood next to one another. Plumes of smoky ash puffed from their open mouths. The largest of the three was a red male. The two smaller ones were also male and had golden scales. Dragon eyes are mystical. Spinning like pinwheels, they're a burnished golden color with deep green centers. I hoped Dariyah had gotten a good look.

I walked to Aedan's side and stood waiting for the dirge to draw to a close. Soir was crying. My heart went out to her. She'd been as much a victim as Rona. Dragon tears form gemstones. Unicorn tears turn to little chunks of gold that match their horns.

"Where have you been?" Aedan bent close to my ear.

"Dealing with Ysir. He was in my quarters and delusional."

Aedan shrugged. "So what else is new?"

I changed the subject to draw his curiosity away from my absence. "Have you been to Fire Mountain?"

"Aye. I went right after we talked about it. The volcanoes hadn't grown worse. My next trip there is scheduled for tomorrow."

"Hmmm. Do you know why the dragons are here?"

Aedan shook his head. "Not a clue."

"I'll be calling an emergency session of court right after this. Spread the word, please."

He looked askance at me, but the questions I saw in his mind didn't emerge from his mouth. Good, because I wouldn't have answered any of them. Not yet. I was still considering how everything slotted together.

I made my way to the dragons and inclined my head. The dirge was winding down. Once it ended, I said, "Welcome, although I fear today is a sad occasion. How may I assist you?"

"Our seers bring tidings," the red dragon intoned. "Rather than carry the information—and miss some of the nuances—I took the liberty of bringing them with me."

The two gold dragons opened scaled lids and swiveled their heads my way. Rather than gold and green, their eyes were a milky white. Blind. They must be blind. It was almost *de rigueur* for seers, as if shutting off their usual manner of sight was required to open psychic channels.

"I've just called an emergency session of the Fae court," I told them. "Please join us. You can share your prophecies and remain if you wish to take part in the ensuing discussion."

"We accept," one of the golds said.

"Will we fit in the room?" the other asked.

"Of course," I told him. "The court chambers were constructed to accommodate all of Faery's subjects."

"We are no one's subjects," the red dragon informed me and covered me with a cloud of smoke that made me cough.

"Oberon made that error," one of the golds said.

"You'd do well not to repeat it," the other chimed in.

"Oberon made a lot of mistakes," I told them. "Follow me inside, and if you could keep the smoke and ash to a minimum—"

"We're housebroken." The red dragon laughed uproariously. Plumes of fiery ash spewed from his mouth.

Glad he had a sense of humor—something I'd never have guessed—I led the way to the castle's massive front doors. The dragons wouldn't have fit through the side entrance I'd used to access the courtyard. Wings spread for balance, they trudged up the broad, shallow steps leading inside.

Like all castles, the interior of Dubrova was designed with the idea of a warrior in full armor riding a horse through its primary corridor. Not that there were horses in Faery. Unicorns only looked like horses.

So far as I knew, they'd never suffered anyone on their backs.

The court chamber opened to the right. I spoke a few words, and the illusory curtain hiding it from view dropped away. I stepped aside and motioned the dragons to go on in. I assumed they'd settle without instructions from me. So far we were the only ones here, but the relative solitude didn't last long. Aedan and the eleven other current delegates trooped in and took their usual spots around a long, U-shaped wooden table, I glanced at the elegant space. Paneled in rare dark wood, it was lit by a row of crystalline windows set high in the far wall. Shelves were piled with the lore scrolls we referred to most often.

Setting a brisk pace, I took my spot at the head of the table. After all this time, it should feel more like mine, but I still felt like a placeholder. I needed to get over that. I scanned the delegates. A rotating task, we traded off every two years. I was the only constant on the court. The current group consisted of half-a-dozen Fae, three Sidhe, one unicorn, and two satyrs. I'd have liked it better if Fae weren't a majority, but delegates were elected by popular vote.

The unicorn whinnied. "Before we begin," he said, "I'm worried about Soir. She's been ramming her horn into trees and rocks since the...accident. She swears she has no memory of the event, and she blames herself. Even though it flies in the face of logic, I believe her."

"If the court is in agreement"—I kept my tone formal—"I would like to include Soir for the first part of what I have to tell you."

"Why?" the unicorn asked. "If it will make her feel guiltier—"

"It won't." I interrupted him. "Do I have special consideration from the court regarding my request?"

Right hands shot up, the universal sign for yes. I felt a jolt of the unicorns' distinctive brand of magic. Moments later the sound of hoofs cantering on wood was followed by Soir's long neck craning through the doorway. The hair around her eyes was matted with tears.

"It's all right. Please enter," I told the unicorn. She made a dash for her kinsman who sat on our court and stood behind him making little snuffling noises that hurt my heart. I draped a sound shield around the chamber. It earned me some surprised looks. We'd never felt the need to protect our discussions from others in Faery, but I wasn't taking any chances.

Because I couldn't tell them about Dariyah, I said, "Earlier, I sensed someone was in my rooms, so I left the funeral to investigate. I found Ysir, more unhinged than usual, and sent him back to the library. So long as I was several floors up—and not likely to disturb the funeral—

I pushed a window open and cast a spell to tap into Rona's memories of her last moments.

A tortured whinny burst from Soir. "I should leave. I'll end myself. No reason for any of the rest of you to waste even one more moment on my misery, and—"

"Do not jump to conclusions." I shook a finger her way. "Hear me out." I hurried to describe the darkness that had descended on the two unicorns, and the result.

Outraged squawks and shouts ran around the courtroom. Above them, I heard Soir. Ears pricked forward, she whinnied, "So it truly wasn't my fault?"

"Nay. It was not. You may go now, but I wanted you to hear the truth for yourself."

"Why'd they pick Rona and me?" she demanded.

"It wasn't specific to the two of you. Murdering a unicorn drives home vicious intent. You have no enemies," I replied.

"We do now," the unicorn who sat on the court muttered. He nudged Soir. "Leave now. Get some rest."

With a toss of her mane, she trotted out of the chamber. I tested the sound shield to make certain my next words would remain within. "The other problem I bring is Oberon. He is far from gone. He hired a mage to spy on me. Actually a series of them. Only reason I know is I apprehended the current one."

"Why bother to spy on you?" Aedan's question held a tortured note. He'd always idolized the Fae king.

"That I do not know," I told him. "Another wrinkle is Titania. She appears to be missing. She isn't with him, like all of us assumed. Have any of you seen or heard from her in, say, the last fifty years or so?"

One of the satyrs stamped his hoofs. He didn't quite hang his head, but neither did he meet my eyes. "She and I, we, uh, well... I was one of her favorites. I figured Oberon found out and forbade further dalliances, but this casts a much darker light on things."

Interesting. It did, indeed.

"We face multiple challenges," I told the group. "The most pressing is finding the one who violated our defenses and is actually running amok in Faery."

"It must be one of us," the unicorn said flatly.

I nodded agreement. The same conclusion had kicked me in the guts when I listened to Dariyah.

"But that's terrible," a female Sidhe cried out. "What are we supposed to do? Quiz our friends? Our relatives? Neighbors we've had for centuries? What if we don't like their answers? Do we quietly turn them in to the court? Or maybe not so quietly."

"Not quietly at all," the other satyr said. "It won't take long until everyone knows we're on the hunt for vigilantes in our midst."

"Which is why we must do this with subtlety." I raised my voice to be heard over the melee. "If word leaks, whoever is responsible will go to ground."

"Wouldn't that solve our problem?" The Sidhe tossed hair over her shoulders.

The unicorn swished his mane in agreement. "We put the word out and watch for who disappears."

"Maybe they disappear," I said. "If they don't, we're back to square one."

"What are you going to do about Oberon?" Aedan asked.

I blew out a tight breath, but it didn't release any tension or alter how shitty I was feeling. "I have no idea, but we can't deal with him until we get the primary problem under control."

"What if he wants to come back?" the unicorn asked. After a pause, he added, "It was a great relief to many of us when his departure became permanent."

"I know." I left it at that. The only ones who hadn't felt threatened by Oberon's policies were other Fae, but labeling him as a racist bastard wasn't productive.

"How does one secure permission to speak?" one of the dragon seers asked.

I hadn't forgotten about them, but making certain to list all our problems had taken center stage. "You have the floor," I told the seer. "I'd planned to hear you first, but the unicorn was in distress. Thank you in advance for traveling all this way to—"

"Once I'm done, you'll curse the day I was hatched." The dragon's voice rustled like dry leaves.

My stomach twisted into a knot; I spun one hand in a circle to encourage him to begin speaking. Faery hadn't been without problems, but they'd been minor for all the millennia since its inception. All that was about to change.

Nay, one of my inner critics corrected me. *It already has.*

The seer turned to his companion, and the two of them blew steam at one another accompanied by a series of clicks, clacks, and muted bugles. I'd never heard their private language before. It was eerie and unnerving.

The one who'd spoken waddled the length of the room until he stood next to where I sat. "I will be brief," he said. "You've already discovered there are enemies in your midst. Aye, more than one. You cannot stop searching until you've ferreted them all out. Oberon is behind this incursion. He never relinquished his hold on Faery. Your land is dying because the regent—and by that I mean you—does not control the link to it. If you cannot rectify this mismatch soon, the world that succors you will wither and die a horrendous death. She is already experiencing pain beyond your worst imaginings and lashing out."

The dragon turned and started to shuffle back to the other two. "If you will," I called after him, "hold a moment."

He swiveled his head atop his long neck. "I have naught more to say. You must fix this."

"Do you know how many enemies reside among us?"

"Nay. Only that there are more than one."

"One more question?" I waited.

"One more, Regent, and then I must be gone."

"Did you mean Oberon is behind the traitors too?"

"Aye. He is angry and powerful. Growing more so with each passing day."

"Why?" a satyr cried.

The dragon shrugged amid rattling scales. "Who can say. He always had his own agenda. It was one of our reasons for not spending overmuch time in Faery during his long reign."

"We report problems. It is not our task to solve them," the other seer had begun moving toward the door accompanied by the red dragon.

"Thank you for telling us." I bowed low before the dragons.

"Anytime," the red dragon said. "We never cared for Oberon. Best of luck finding a way to eliminate him. Let us know if you require our assistance."

"We did not come here out of a sense of misplaced altruism," one of the seers said.

"We most certainly did not," the other added. "If Faery dies, so does Fire Mountain, and we will lose our precious home."

I waited until the dragons had left and looked from one crestfallen, dejected mage to the next. None of us welcome disputes or tension. It was a good starting point. "Conflict doesn't come naturally to us," I began, "but we cannot turn our backs on this problem."

"No one said we were going to." A Fae sounded surly.

"The floor is open. Before we leave this room, we will have developed an overarching plan to identify and eradicate the traitors," I said and waited. It took a long while before anyone spoke up, and an even longer one before the bones of a viable strategy began to emerge.

CHAPTER NINE, DARIYAH

Dragons! I still couldn't believe I'd seen dragons. Noble and majestic, with incredible wingspans, they'd captivated me. As I broke through the veil between Faery and Earth, I recreated them in my mind again and again. What would it be like to talk with one? To ride on a dragon's back? Did they ever accept riders? If the lore books were to be believed, a scant handful of rare mages had ridden one.

I corrected course, returning to the spot I'd searched for the rift. I wasn't certain how time flowed in Faery, but my guess was it would be far too early to apartment hunt. At least today, the two worlds appeared to share a timeclock. Dawn was breaking as I walked through my spell and emerged near the far point of last night's exploration.

A bevy of raucous bleating accompanied by heavy hoofs churning up mud suggested I'd scared the crap out of a small herd of mountain goats. "It's all right," I called and sent calming vibrations outward, but they were a quarter of a mile away by then. Damn. They moved fast when they wanted to.

Driven by a new urgency, I picked up where I'd left off and walked due north along the base of cliff-riddled foothills. I'd let my attention linger on the dragons because the scene in the dead unicorn's mind had been so upsetting. I wished Cyn and his court well as they crafted plans to address the disaster before it claimed more souls and more magic.

Deep in thought, a blistering bit of insight brought me up short, and I slapped a palm against my forehead. Talk about missing the obvious. I hadn't checked, but I felt certain whoever had orchestrated the deadly charade had drained Rona's magic to strengthen themselves.

I punched the cliff. Fuckers. The side with the most magic was sure to win; they'd probably been systematically draining everyone they came into contact with. Oberon had tippled from me like as not, but he'd been subtle about it. Or maybe he'd turned up his nose at Witch magic. It's viewed as inferior with its reliance on charms.

If I ever saw him again, I'd take care to build a wall around my magical center.

Longing swept through me. For Faery. For Cynwrigg. To finally be what I should have been born into. I was sick of skulking on the sidelines, of pretending to be a Witch. Not that there's anything wrong with Witches. I could have picked any iteration of mage but had settled on Witches because of their commitment to sisterhood.

If I had my way, I'd retire my habitual glamour, lay it aside. I wanted to fight for Faery. It had been my magic that had raked through Rona's memories. Mine!

No one else had thought to do such a simple thing. Maybe not simple. It had taken a buttload of magic, but the casting itself was straightforward. I'd stopped walking, and I urged myself to keep going, pausing every few feet to check the integrity of the boundary.

I could do a lot of good in Faery. They needed me. They—

"Stop. Just stop." I spoke out loud to emphasize my words. Faery had gotten along very nicely, thank you, without my august presence. To talk myself into them requiring me now was the worst kind of hubris and posed a major risk to Mother.

Something about the hole I'd just drilled into the cliff didn't feel right, but I was too wound up to be on top of my game. Sinking into a crouch, I splayed my hands against smooth, cool granite and drew power from the earth beneath my feet and the stone under my fingertips.

Clearing my mind of everything, I focused on breathing. Just breathing until my single-minded obsession with returning to Faery retreated. I could have gone there anytime all these years. I'd stayed away out of respect for Mother. She'd sacrificed her life so I'd have one. Marching into Faery hadn't been particularly smart, even under Cyn's watchful eyes. If I'd been detected, Mother would have felt the ripples as life left my body.

Brave words. Noble, even, but I suspected I'd return as soon as an opportunity presented itself, no matter what the downside entailed. My observations—and my magic—had been a huge help. Despite my short stay, the place had gotten its hooks into me, and I longed to spend much more time than I had.

Meh. I was at it again. Mind-fucking myself to dredge up righteous reasons to go back.

"They do not need me." I repeated myself. "They do not need me. I might need Faery, but I'm stronger than this."

I said it a few more times in a failed attempt to make myself believe it. If I'd realized a quick transit through my homeland would have spawned such angst, I'd never have accepted Cyn's offer...

Bullshit. My favorite internal commentator was back. *Yeah, I would have because he fascinates me. I was flattered by the invitation. No way would I have turned it down. The issue is what will I do next time?*

Wincing, I forced myself to think about the question I'd posed. The wisest move would be no more Faery until they altered their longstanding policy about killing those like me. Cynwrigg would do his best to shield me, but if we were caught, his days as regent would be numbered.

The best thing for us both would be for me to strap on a set and say no. And mean it. He'd understand. He'd asked me because he was smitten, not because it had been wise.

Now that I had that little snippet straight, I stood and moved my hands up the wall as I searched for the spot that hadn't felt quite like all the other ones. I could have imagined it, but it was worth a second look.

Yes! I probed up, down, and sideways, identifying three places where my power bounced back at me differently. Drawing a protective shield around myself, I prepared to enter the cliff to investigate, but then I remembered Cyn's instructions.

I was supposed to find him. His reasoning had been Faery would be appalled by my mixed blood, and it would make things worse. Standing in place, fingertips still glued to the wall, I considered it. I'd been in Faery. The land hadn't reacted at all. Cyn seemed to think it had accepted me, but I had no idea how he'd come to that conclusion. Might have been wishful thinking, but perhaps he'd been right. Otherwise, my presence would have spawned a far greater reaction than what I'd sensed.

The more I played it back and forth, the fewer reasons emerged on the side of waiting until I could alert Cynwrigg. His plate was full, overflowing. This was a small potatoes operation. I'd go in, have a peek, see if this place really led to the rift, and if it appeared amenable to closure from this angle. Once I had a few answers, then I'd hunt Cyn down.

It should have decided things, but I remained mid spell, still debating if I was being smart. I'd given Cyn my word I wouldn't do this. The argument "he'll never know" didn't apply since I'd tell him everything I found.

I shook my head to clear it. What in the hell was wrong with me? I wasn't a coward, not by a longshot. If he couldn't accept that I'd done something in the interest of making his life a little easier, we had zero future together. I've never been the type to wait for anyone to give me permission to move forward, and I wasn't about to start now.

Gathering the tattered edges of my casting, I wrapped myself in a version of a teleport spell and ordered it to move me inside the rock wall. If I was correct, the inside would be hollow and lead to the space between worlds. I'd been to a few of those over the years.

It might have been part of my reluctance. The holes

between worlds were singularly unpleasant. If I were just traversing it, all I'd feel would be a slight tug at the transitional point. But I needed to aim for its center and examine it. A ghostly wind howled, whipping around me. Something clattered alarmingly; hail pelted me with sharp particles about the time I figured out what was making the racket.

At least I'd been right about the hollow part. No wind or hail inside solid rock. My eyes were wide open, but the space was pitch black. I tried my third eye with no better success before giving up and bringing a mage light to life. I kept it muted in case I wasn't alone. I hadn't sensed anyone else, but many things can conceal their power.

A flickering candle appeared far less threatening than a floodlight, and my goal was convincing someone I was harmless. Most assumed weak light equaled weak magic. A cavern came into view around me. Peppered with stalagmites and stalactites formed from coal-black rocks, it was narrower than I'd expected. Shielding my eyes from both wind and hail, I perched on a rocky outcropping since the cave had no lower surface. In its place sat a jagged schism that had to be what I hunted.

Water was everywhere. Dripping, rushing, cascading through the bottom of the raggedy opening where a strip of dirt should have been. I felt the pull of Earth from behind me, and the inexorable draw of Faery from the other side of the rift. Low moaning joined the wind, the sound so full of misery it gutted me.

I wanted to help, but I had no idea what to do. I returned my attention to the ruptured spot, assessing how much magic it would take to draw the edges together. In the spirit of collecting as much information as possible, I sent a tentative thread of enchantment to the far side of the gorge and spoke the word, "Close," in a very old form of Gaelic.

Mother trained me to weave magic. We had nothing but time, and she was a strict taskmistress. She'd taught me this spell. Had she known I'd need it one day? Anything was possible. She was clairvoyant as hell. Her skill had allowed her to stay two steps ahead of the Fae pursuing us until they finally gave up.

The wind shrieked louder. I grabbed hold of my perch so I wouldn't end up blown off it. My pants were wet through from the rock. Probably nothing was ever dry in here. Hail pelted me, sharp as knife points. I tugged my jacket over my head, but it was woefully inadequate.

I dialed up the lumens on my light and peered at the spot I'd targeted. Yeehaw! What I'd done had worked. A land bridge about two feet wide spanned the schism. Afraid it would break apart if I didn't add to my good work, I sent more magic to the same spot. This time, instead of "Close," I said, "Grow."

Totally unprepared for what happened next, I scrambled to reverse my spell. Breath swooshed from me. The harder I tried, the worse things became. Power rushed out of my core as surely as if someone had installed a spigot dead center in my magic. The land bridge expanded by leaps and bounds. That part was great, but I couldn't keep this up. I'd end up running on fumes without sufficient magic to crawl back to Earth.

I tried several things to modulate the outflow of magic. Nothing made the slightest difference. Panic rode me like a deranged hag, too close to the surface for comfort. I began to shiver; my breath came fast making clouds in the chilly air. The wind still pummeled me, but it had quit hailing.

Could I stop the spell?

It sure wasn't looking that way. Someone liked what I'd done, and they wouldn't be satisfied until they took everything I had. From the looks of things, I might barely have enough power left to close the gap. Whether the fix would be permanent was anyone's guess, but it wouldn't matter if I ended up stranded down here, cut off from the place I regenerated my power.

No matter how bleak things appeared, I had to try to stem the outflow while I still could. I shouted, "End." Then I shouted, "Stop."

An answering, "Nooooo, you are mine. You are

finally mine again to heal my hurts. I will release you when I choose.”

“I was never yours. You are mistaken.” I tried again to clip the cords that bound me to that infernal hole. An opening that had reduced itself by perhaps three-quarters. A quick internal assessment told me I had nothing left to spare. Whoever was pulling the strings was parceling out my power in such a way I’d be done when the chasm was closed.

“You are mine! It is why you came to heal me,” the gravelly voice, lacking gender clues, continued.

“I came to see if you could be healed,” I corrected whatever was talking to me. “The first bridge was an experiment. I can finish this, but you must allow me to pace myself.”

“You hold sufficient magic. I checked.”

“So did I,” I replied acidly. “But once you’re done, I will be trapped here.”

“Your magic will recover.”

“No. Not here it won’t.” I was panting. My heart beat like a tripwire as power cascaded from me. It wasn’t the magic leaving that ate at me, but my dread about sitting out the next several millennia in this wet, rocky cave.

“You are mine,” the voice repeated. “I will tend to you because you succored me. No one else cared. The ones who should have abandoned me.”

Before I could push my frantic brain to spit out an

argument that might earn my freedom, the drain on my ability doubled and then trebled. The hand I'd been clinging to my roost with let go, but I was beyond caring. The next blast of wind tossed me into the void. At least I wouldn't fall through the chasm into the river, but I had no magic left to cushion my fall.

I expected to hit hard enough to break bones. No magic left to fix those, either. Jesus. I was so fucked. Why hadn't I listened to Cyn?

Because I'm too goddamned independent for my own good. Even my inner voice was weak, disconnected. I waited for impact, for the splat that would send pain ratcheting through my body.

I might have blacked out, but it never came. Instead, I floated on a blanket of air. The wind was gone, and the cave had warmed a few degrees. Didn't matter, I shivered hard enough my teeth rattled against each other. Had the voice belonged to Faery? It almost had to.

Who else had a pony in this race?

The floating sensation was pleasant. I was empty, tapped out, worthless as a mage, but I didn't care. For once I stopped trying to control everything. It would have been ridiculous since I wasn't on top of anything. I should have been panic-stricken to be at the mercy of whoever had woven the soft blanket beneath my head and body, but I couldn't locate even a shred of resistance.

"Thank you for not killing me," I murmured.

"Thank you for healing me, daughter of my bones."

The scene shifted so fast I had no idea what happened. The cavern broke apart. In its place stood the base of the rocky cliff where I'd first sensed this might be the spot to hunt for the rift.

My knees buckled, and I sank to the rock-strewn earth, breathing as if I'd just run a race. How in the hell was I not terminally broken? What had the voice meant by daughter of my bones? If it had been Faery, she'd have recognized me as anathema, as something to be snuffed out. And she'd certainly had plenty of opportunity. She could have stolen my magic and left me for the crows or the fish or whatever lived in that subterranean chasm.

I crossed my legs under me and rubbed my temples. I had a mother of a headache. Big surprise given all the power I'd burned through. Power. Did I have enough left to teleport, or would I be relegated to walking to the nearest road and hitchhiking? I had no other resources at my disposal. No purse. No phone. No money.

No need for any of those in magical worlds, but a person couldn't get along without them here. I stopped thinking about what I didn't have and focused my mind inward.

Yes! Fuck, yes! I wasn't totally dry. My first stop had to be the in between place where I tanked up. It would take a while, but that didn't matter. I was tired. I'd teleport there, open my tapped-out magical center, and take a nap. By the time I was done, there'd still be an hour or two to score a new spot to live. I wasn't totally clear how I'd move my few possessions, but if I left them it wouldn't be the end of the world. I'd started over so many times I'd lost count.

Oberon had probably posted sentries around my place 24/7. I hoped Midnight was okay. He was tough and had good instincts. From what I'd seen of Oberon's flunkies, it wouldn't be much of a contest. The thought made me smile, but it faded fast.

Cyn would know what I'd done, probably knew already. Or he'd realize someone had stepped in, and the most likely candidate was me. Breath hissed from between my teeth. At least I'd finally quit shivering. My clothes wouldn't be dry for a while, but midday in northern Nevada was quite warm this time of year.

For a moment, I'd been flirting with covering up what I'd done. Ha! As if I could. Everyone's power has a particular signature. Mine was bleeding all over this operation. Nope. I'd have to fess up. As regent, Cynwrigg had a right to know. Hell, as regent, I owed him.

The concept rocked me. Other than Mother, I'd never owed anyone jack.

Slowly, creakily, I got to my feet. Interestingly, the small amount of power left in me was actually expanding. It shouldn't be able to do that, not without a trip to the in-between place.

Shaking my head, I set a spell in motion, taking care to be as sparing as I could with how I finessed it. I had boatloads of questions, but not a single answer. They'd have to wait. Once Cyn got through reading me the riot act—and he would—he might have an idea or two.

If he was still speaking to me.

I had a feeling most of his subjects were more compliant. The notion of me and compliant sharing the same clump of words made me laugh. I was still laughing as my spell swept me away from the cliffs to the soothing darkness of the in between.

✻ 10 ✻

CHAPTER TEN, CYN

Court had lasted forever, but we were finally winding down when a jolt began in my toes and rocked me, nearly knocking me out of my chair. Certain we were under attack from somewhere, I leapt to my feet shouting, "What was that?"

"Don't know." Aedan picked himself up off the floor.

The unicorn and satyrs stamped their hoofs, and a satyr cried, "The vigilantes who murdered Rona might be back in force."

It seemed remote, but I wasn't discounting any possibilities. Faery was turning to shit under my nose. I couldn't afford to make any more mistakes.

"We are done here," I told everyone. "You have your assignments. I'll scan for threats. I know where to find you if I need you."

"Will you still be splitting your time between here and Earth?" a satyr asked.

"I will be here as much as I can. There's still the rift to deal with. It didn't go away just because we've been invaded."

He nodded in understanding, and maybe sympathy, before trotting out of the room, hoofs clicking on the wooden floor. Eh, sympathy was a major exaggeration. Satyrs are many things, but empathy isn't in their wheelhouse. I waited for another jolt, for Dubrova castle to devolve into a pile of rocks and glass, but it never came.

Meanwhile, I sent power zinging in a full circle, searching for hazards. Faery didn't feel any different, but she might not, given my lack of a link with her.

Everyone had left. I didn't blame them; we'd been at it for hours. For all the years of my memory the Fae court had been more pomp and circumstance than actual function. We'd heard the occasional case, and meted out rare punishments, but our meetings were more social than judicial. Planning the next festival was far more common—and pleasant—than strategizing to fix something broken.

After pulling my notes together—mostly lists of who was responsible for what—I walked slowly from the courtroom. I should check on Faery, on the rift, to make certain whatever rolled through hadn't injured her further. Had Dariyah located Earth's side of the schism?

I hastened my pace. The shockwave might have been Faery's fury at a hybrid daring to show her face in anyplace related to her enchanted world.

Dariyah had gotten away with her brief tryst in my chamber, but I keep my rooms swathed in spells. Between them and her glamour, it was quite possible Faery hadn't questioned the Witch glamour and had placed her mark of acceptance on Dariyah. Unfortunately, the Fae-Sidhe hybrid wouldn't have had my rooms' protections on a solo endeavor.

It might have made a huge difference.

I'd broken into a run, and then I drew up short. This was ridiculous. I'd teleport to the subterranean spot where the rift was and take it from there. Meanwhile, I had to be overreacting all over the bloody place. Dariyah had given me her word she'd only do a reconnaissance. If she found something, she'd let me know.

All that had been before we discovered perfidy within Faery's boundaries... I cleared my mind of everything and set a course for the spot where I tried to talk with the land. My usual location shimmered into being. I glanced around and blinked a few times. How had I made such a monumental error. This wasn't the right place at all.

Dirt spread beneath my feet in all directions. No hole. No rift. No chasm. Crap. I must be more exhausted than I'd thought to make such a rookie mistake. Shutting my eyes, I breathed a few times to center myself, and then cast the same spell.

Nothing happened. When I opened both my normal eyes and my third eye to double-check, I still stood in the same spot. The only reason that could have happened was because my first attempt hadn't failed after all.

Where was the rift?

I darted forward, testing each step with magic. In case the smooth surface in front of me was an illusion, I didn't want to fall through. My nostrils twitched as I scented the air, hunting clues. I walked the line where the rift had spread in both directions. Long before I was done, I recognized Dariyah's hand in the miracle stretching around me.

Anger sparred with gratitude, creating an eerie, confusing mélange. She'd broken her word, which meant I could never trust her. But she'd cured the rift, sewed it together seamlessly from what I could ascertain. Faced with the extent of her power, I felt ashamed and petty. She'd turned her talents to mend a land that had spurned her.

By rights, she should have walked away. I still didn't understand why she was helping me at all, but I'd never seen the like of her ability. The dragons' prophecy about my lack of a bond with Faery—and its consequences— nagged for recognition.

Bowing low, I said, "It is such a relief to find you whole, my lady. I am here for you. You need only reach out." So long as I was talking, I continued, "Your boundaries have been breached by wickedness. I am doing my best to ferret out the miscreants."

A wave of unpleasantness flew through the cavern, followed by another. The sensation set my teeth on edge as I sought to interpret what was behind it. "Talk with me," I pleaded. "I can't help if I don't know what's wrong."

The next blast of air smelled like Dariyah. I inhaled hungrily, craving her and furious with myself at the same time. I couldn't trust her. No matter how great a boon she'd performed for Faery, her word was meaningless. It was smallminded of me, but I couldn't seem to move past it. My pride was hurt because she'd obviously decided she didn't need me. At all.

Grasping at straws, I tried again to talk with Faery, "I know that scent, and I assume Dariyah was the hand behind your miraculous recovery. I shall thank her for you."

The air currents stilled. No clues there. I waited, but once again the land had no interest in talking. Frustration twisted my empty stomach into a knot. I curled one hand into a fist and drove it into a rocky wall, skinning my knuckles. "I am not Oberon," I growled. "I will never be him, nor do I wish to be. Beyond that, he will never return. You must sever the bond, so I can pick up the reins and be Faery's regent in more than name only."

"She will never do that," a familiar voice echoed. "Because I won't let her."

"Oberon!" I shouted, scanning with magic and my eyes but not seeing him. "Your greed will be the death of Faery."

"That's for me to decide. She is mine," he said smoothly.

"Show yourself," I demanded. "Only cowards hide in shadows or behind magical shields."

Harsh, bitter laughter pelted me, fading by the minute.

"That's right," I bellowed after his retreat. "Run, you craven bastard. The universe isn't big enough to conceal you forever. When I find you, you're a dead man." I uncurled fingers that had fisted of their own accord, longing to bash his patrician face in. I could almost hear the sound of bones breaking, crunchy and satisfying.

One thing he'd spat my way sank in. "He said you're barred from talking with me," I tossed out. "If it's true, do something."

A disturbance rippled the currents blowing through this spot. I heard whistling and feinted left moments before a small boulder crashed to the ground. *Alrighty, then.* For all Oberon's faults, with arrogance leading the list, I'd never known him to be a liar. Twisting the truth happened frequently, but not out-and-out lies.

"Thank you," I told Faery. "I will do my best to sever the hold he has on you." Insight banged home. "The rift. It was your way of flagging my attention, wasn't it?"

Two more stones plunked down, coming to rest a short distance from my boots. Excuses crowded the back of my throat; I swallowed them all. Faery may have been a peaceful spot, a safe haven, for time untold. Because of its uneventful history, I'd expected it to remain so. The blinders were off. I'd been wrong to make excuses for every departure from what used to be normal. If I'd been quicker on the uptake, more alert to subtle alterations, I might have stepped in before events progressed to this point.

A big part of my problem was my failure to embrace my position as regent. Unlike many others, I'd never longed for leadership. I'd been disappointed when Faery voted to ratify Oberon's line of succession. The way our covenant is structured, the people could have suggested other names to place on the ballot. No one did.

They liked me. I was a known quantity. No one ever thought they'd need a leader, and like the unicorn had said—out loud—many had been relieved to see Oberon and his heavy-handed ways depart.

A bitter laugh rattled through me. They'd been delighted to see him go, but I'd been half-hoping he'd come back and fix the rift so I wouldn't have to spend so much time on Earth. I'd established détente with my role at Lady Luck, but the endless procession of hookers and gamblers and wannabe gangsters dragged at me. One thing about gambling towns, they attracted society's dregs like moths clung to burning candles.

"I'll do everything I can for you," I promised Faery, "just as soon as I find the vigilantes and string them up." I paused, gathering my thoughts. Talking with Faery was like talking to a sentient wall. She couldn't answer, but she was the best of listeners.

"The traitors will be people I know," I went on. "Ending them will pound stakes into my soul, but it will set an example for everyone else. Any of Faery's residents who are inclined to sabotage the land that supports them can leave. It will be a one-time-only offer."

Power bubbled around me as I left the hobbled land to her anger. Was it only me she couldn't talk with? Or had Oberon stolen her voice with everyone? One thing was almost a given. Once she broke free, she'd flatten him and crush his link with her.

I'd been a fool. Events had unfolded in plain sight with me oblivious. I couldn't rewrite history. No magic was strong enough to accomplish that, but I could institute solutions from here on. My rooms came into focus around me. After a quick shower, I donned fresh clothes. No one had reached out for me, which meant no new information to chase down. I raised my mind voice. *"Aedan."*

He replied immediately. *"Aye, Regent."*

I blinked a couple of times. He rarely addressed me by my title. Must mean he was rattled by the turn of events. Oberon had been far more of a father figure to him than to me. I'd never liked the old fucker while Aedan had appeared blind to his faults.

"Join me," I told him.

He must have anticipated my command. Seconds later, a knock sounded on my door. I tugged it open and stepped aside for him to enter. His usual impeccable level of tailoring had slipped a little. Lines around his eyes suggested he was worried.

"No word from the court," he said before I could ask.

"It hasn't been very long," I reminded him. "These things take time."

A muscle danced beneath one of his silver eyes. "I want this to be over. I still can't believe Oberon is a traitor. There has to be another reason Titania is missing too. She had a habit of going off on retreats. It's probably where—"

"Spa days don't last fifty years. Get over it," I snapped, breaking into his tumble of words. "I was just with Faery. The rift is healed, and—"

"See?" Triumph underscored the one word. "Told you. Oberon fixed it. He's the only one with power to manage such a feat."

"Try again," I suggested silkily.

"Fuck you, Cyn. You never liked him, and you'll jump on any excuse to sully his name."

Temper dangerously thin, I made a grab for his forearm. "Net me in a truth spell. Do it now."

After rolling his eyes, a pallid excuse for a truth spell dropped over my head. "You can do better than that," I told my cousin.

"This will do," he mumbled.

After testing its sloppy construction, I bit back criticism and hoped to holy hell his magic wasn't representative of the rest of Faery. When had his skills grown so slipshod?

I tightened my grip on his arm. "A woman I met on Earth, a mage, has been helping me. She's who healed the rift."

"You sent a stranger?" Aedan was aghast.

"Nay. Her task was to find the schism on Earth's side, not to mend it, but I assume she experimented with something, discovered it worked, and finished the job." I gave his arm a shake. "You're missing the point. There is no more rift. Faery created it to get my attention. She can't talk. Oberon stole her voice."

"Pfft. How could you possibly know that?"

I grabbed his other arm, shook him harder, and stared him down. "Have you been paying attention to your truth spell? It pings a certain—"

Aedan tried to yank free of my grip, but I held fast. "I do not require magical instruction from you," he gritted.

"You require it from someone," I shot back. "I've never seen such sloppy spell-work from a grown-up. Kids, sure, but not a fully vetted mage."

He ignored my criticism. "If Faery can't talk, there's no way she could have told you anything." He simpered my way. For the first time, I doubted which side my cousin was on.

"I asked her questions," I told him. "She answered in her own manner, but one that left no doubt."

"Your interpretation. Nothing more. Let me go."

I waited a beat to allow my next words to sink in. "I also know because Oberon showed up and told me he'd hobbled Faery so she couldn't talk with me."

"You're flat out lying," he snarled, showing me a mouthful of teeth.

"Not according to your truth spell." Startled by his lack of competence as a mage, I released his arms. "I must leave. I'll return as quickly as I can." I'd meant to place him in charge of our undertaking, but it felt like an exceedingly bad idea. Perhaps I'd begun seeing boogeymen under beds, but I didn't trust my cousin as far as I could see him.

"Fine. I'll go talk with Faery. See if I can't get to the bottom of this."

Something about the way he said it chilled me. "You'll do no such thing. She's struggling."

"You won't be here," he taunted me.

My next move was pure instinct. Leveraging magic, I dropped a cage over his head and wound streamers around it to block telepathy. Satisfied it would hold him, I sealed it with power only I could dismantle. "Maybe not," I replied, "but you will remain in this spot until I free you. I just made certain of it."

He screamed epithets, shouted I'd lost my marbles. I added a sound shield around his temporary prison. As soon as I was done, I left for Earth. I'd have to justify my actions with Aedan. Normally, detaining anyone required a vote from the court.

There hadn't been time.

Oberon had broken all our rules. Time for me to stop being a Goody Two-shoes and break a few of my own. The name made me smile. I'd known her. What a little bitch she'd been. Nicey-nice on the surface, but totally self-serving beneath her veneer.

The stairwell beneath Lady Luck came into view. I took the steps two at a time. When I hit ground level and got a peek through an outside window, afternoon was on the wane. I raised my mind voice to call Dariyah. She didn't answer, but it wasn't a complete surprise.

She'd assume I was furious with her. Or maybe she was asleep. Even with her level of ability, she must have burned herself down to cinders closing the rift. I didn't see how she'd managed it. I would have required additional power to accomplish the same task. Still thinking about her, overawed by her sheer talent, I continued upward to my office. After unlocking my desk and freeing my electronic jungle of devices, I worked my way through a pile of notes.

At some point, dinner arrived from the kitchen. I wasn't picky, so I'd told them to surprise me. Tonight's offering was beef with garlic sauce, jasmine rice, a thinly sliced pork dish, and an assortment of raw fish presented sashimi style. I finished the food and all my work at the same time. It wouldn't be dark for a while yet. Should I hunt for Dariyah or leave her alone?

I tried telepathy again. Shock roiled through me when her deep contralto voice replied, *"Yeah. I'm back topside."*

I started to ask where she'd been, but it was none of my business. Instead, I said, *"Thanks for what you did."*

"You're not mad? I figured you'd be furious."

I chuckled. *"I was, until I thought things through. I would like to hear what happened."* I stopped there. She'd done both me and Faery a huge favor. If she wished to keep the details private, I wouldn't pry.

"*I'm in the middle of renting a new place. Give me maybe an hour.*"

"*How's your cat?*"

"*Thanks for asking. He's fine. He's with me in a carrier.*"

"*If you need help with moving...*"

After a long pause, she said, "*It would be useful if you could dissuade Oberon's spies from following me. If I can't do that, I won't be able to move anything. They'll just track me to the new location, and I'll have done all this work for nothing.*"

"*Come here when you're done. We'll crack a few skulls and move everything with magic.*"

"*You got it. Jeez, I assumed you'd never speak to me again. I've never been so glad to be wrong.*"

"*I have a funny habit of not reaming people who do me favors. See you soon.*"

I broke the connection, rang for the kitchen to pick up my empty plates, and strode out of my office. It was good for my staff to see me on the various gaming floors. Kept them honest. The patrons too. I had a well-deserved reputation for being a hard ass, but a fair one. If problems cropped up, I rarely waited for the cops. Easy enough to toss someone outside onto the asphalt. A quick photo ensured they'd never be allowed within again.

Usually, I started in the basement, but the strains of

"Mendelssohn's Wedding March" reached into the stair-well. I exited on the first floor and wandered over to our small chapel. No waiting to marry in Nevada. It lent new meaning to the old saw about marrying in haste.

Tonight's couple wasn't the norm. Garbed in a flowing gown and tuxedo, they'd clearly planned this. Guests lined the chapel and overflowed into the hall. Normally, I paid scant heed to mortals and their insipid customs, but I wished these two well. Hovering on the outskirts of the ceremony, I stayed until the rice-throwing began before heading downstairs.

The wedding made me think of Dariyah, which was ridiculous. Fae didn't marry, and her mixed blood made her a target in Faery. I cared about her, but not enough to tether myself to Earth forever, and—

I cut through my messy thoughts, bringing them to an abrupt halt. I was so far ahead of the curve, it was absurd. Chances of her and me forging a path that allowed us to become a couple were as nonexistent as the possibility my gamblers would win against the house. Like all casinos, my games were rigged. People could win, but only if they knew when to quit.

"Isn't that the way of everything," I mumbled as I moved from one game room to another. "Gotta know when to fold, or the house will come tumbling down."

CHAPTER ELEVEN, DARIYAH

Keys in hand, I folded my brand-new lease agreement, shook hands with the property management dude who'd been trying to get into my pants from the moment I showed up, and walked briskly into gathering dusk. Midnight yowled piteously in his carrier. He was probably hungry and thirsty, but I wanted to give the dude a few minutes to clear out of my apartment before I went back inside.

Cats don't tend to like new places, so I'd keep Midnight with me until I had a few hours to spend in our new digs. On the west side of Reno, the apartment complex was in a better neighborhood than my old one. Needless to say, the rent was far more than the pittance I'd been paying for my slummy flat.

"We'll make this work," I told my feline buddy after

another series of pathetic growls. "You'll like it, but you have to give it a chance." Another long, drawn-out *mwrowww* suggested Midnight wasn't convinced.

I doubled back to my new place. The agent had indeed left. He might have had a hard-on, but he wasn't stupid. He'd known I had zero interest in him. Like most spurned men, he'd probably chalked me up as gay, which suited me fine. It meant he wouldn't bother calling or texting.

I let myself inside and walked through my two bedrooms, two baths, and a granite kitchen. This place had been built as condominiums, but the bottom had fallen out of the condo market, which was why they'd turned the non-owner units into rentals.

I decided to buy new furniture. It would simplify moving. None of what I had in the old place was worth the effort to transport it. I'd been surprised when Cyn offered to help. Hell, I'd been ecstatic after hearing from him. All my fears had apparently been for naught.

Normally, I didn't waste energy on what-ifs, but he was important to me. If I were honest, it was scary how he'd slithered into center stage in my life. I couldn't bounce in and out of Faery, though, much as I wanted to. The place fascinated me and left me hungry for more.

The thought made me smile. The same could be said of Cynwrigg.

No reason to maintain the charade of being human, so I let Midnight out of his carrier, located a plastic bin under one of the sinks, and filled it with water for him. Nothing I could do about food just now, and I doubted this apartment would offer the varied assortment of mice he'd come to rely on. Not inside, but perhaps over by the dumpsters.

"I'll buy you some cat food," I reassured him.

He looked up from his water and showed me his teeth. I sent a bit of calming magic his way. At least there wasn't any furniture for him to hide beneath, and it would take him a while to find a way out of here—if one existed. The other place was old and full of spaces where the owner had slapped two-by-fours over exterior holes.

Before my house-hunting jaunt, I'd slipped inside my flat long enough to shower and change clothes. Nothing fancy. Dark trousers, a stretchy multihued shirt, and a black jacket. I'd been quick and stealthy. Oberon's spies —three of them again—hadn't reacted. Either they hadn't realized I'd snuck inside, or they were awaiting orders from the fuhrer that never came.

Why did he give a rat's ass about me? I was nobody.

Yeah, a nobody who's bested him over and over again. My inner critic sounded satisfied for once. Praise from her was rare, and I basked in it. My mistake had been not taking the half wages that were offered and walking away. Even if I could relive that decision, I'd do the same thing. Being cheated and turning the other cheek aren't part of my makeup.

I'd thrown down a gauntlet. He'd picked it up, and now we were mortal enemies. I had a feeling he had a long memory. Staying one step ahead of him for the next few centuries would piss me off. Eventually, we'd have it out again and probably sooner rather than later.

The hour I'd estimated when talking with Cyn had more than elapsed. I snatched Midnight and set a teleport spell in motion as the cat writhed, hissed, and spat in my arms. "It's okay. This part never lasts long," I murmured in soothing tones. Not willing to risk a ward since I had no reliable way to muffle the kitty, I set my spell to spit me out in Cynwrigg's office. Except I had to remember to call him Jed if anyone else was there.

If anyone else happened to be there, me popping out of nowhere would take ten years off their life and require a small mind wipe. Too late now. I could redirect my spell, but I didn't want to. Longing to see Cyn was a physical ache right behind my breastbone.

I had to get a serious grip. We were comrades. Fellow soldiers with a common enemy. And we lusted after one another. I licked my lower lip. We could do something about that last part, but was it wise? Sex with him wouldn't quell the heat that ignited every time I laid eyes on him. It would only kick the door open and make me want more.

My spell ran true, but then most of them did. The walls of Cyn's office formed around me. His empty office. So far, so good. Midnight yowled, so I put him down. He ran to the place the empty tuna can had been and looked at me as if to ask where it had gone.

"You good here for a bit?" I asked.

A tail swish as he turned away did double duty as a yes. Before he changed his mind, I snapped my glamour back into place, let myself out the door, and scanned with magic to find Cyn. It would save me a lot of time since the casino was a huge, sprawling affair spread over four floors. I could have saved myself the trouble since he burst from a stairwell with an exit sign flashing over it.

It might be coincidence. More likely he'd set a marker to alert him when I showed up. Maybe I was flattering myself. If I were him, I'd set beacons to alert me if anyone magical breached my gates.

Fuck me. He was even more gorgeous than I remembered—if it was even possible. Flaxen hair with coppery highlights flowed down his back. Tan trousers encased his long legs, and a Romani-style dark-blue shirt set off his eyes. His glamour added girth to his rangy build, but he was stunning either way.

He'd crossed the distance to where I stood,

starstruck like a teenaged girl, and extended his hands. I gripped them just before he crushed me against him, arms winding around my back. I craved his embrace, hungered for the press of his body against mine. Already distended, his cock jammed into my stomach.

"You are so lovely," he murmured.

"Not as pretty as you." I grinned up at him. "Not as tall, either."

He smiled back. "You'd still be hot as a Valkyrie. Come on." Not letting go of me, he walked me backward to his office. The door opened, courtesy of his magic. Midnight raced out, stopped dead, turned, and stalked back inside tail high as he attempted to recoup his dignity.

Cyn kicked the door shut and strung kisses down the side of my face. His erection still tantalized where it was jammed against my belly. Turning my face at the perfect kissing angle was tempting as hell, but we had work ahead of us. Probably lots of it. Too much to lose myself in ripping his clothes off and marveling at the body beneath.

"We need to talk," I murmured, "and you're making it damnably difficult. Odd things happened when I closed the rift, and I didn't actually mean to finish the job. My magic escaped my control. I figured I was a dead woman, but—"

He unwound his arms and dragged a chair over with

a booted foot. "Sit. I'll get us something to drink." Turning, he opened the small refrigerator and asked, "Wine? Beer? Mineral water? Juice?"

"Juice. Any kind. And mineral water and a glass. I'll mix them."

I settled into the chair he'd positioned for me, but it didn't last long. I was too amped up to remain still. Back on my feet, I poured pineapple juice and fizzy water into a glass and took a long sip. Cyn wheeled the chair out from behind his desk and sat across from my empty one, so I sank back into it. I'll hand it to him. He was patient. Didn't pepper me with questions.

I set my glass on the floor. Midnight raced over and stuck his snout in it, lapping until he decided cats didn't like pineapple. My thoughts were as organized as they were likely to get. I'd decided on short, sweet, and no excuses. Spreading my hands in front of me, I began by saying, "I owe you an apology. I broke my word. I didn't mean to. I found a spot that felt promising, so I teleported beyond the cliff and found what I expected, Earth's side of the rift with the unmistakable lure of Faery on the other side.

"It was a strange place, full of wind and hail and colder than I'd have imagined. A river rushed through the bottom of the gorge. My first move, once I determined I was in the right spot, was an experiment to see how tough the gap would be to shut."

I sat straighter in the chair and dropped my hands into my lap. "I agonized over that choice because I remembered our agreement. Aw hell, I vacillated over breaching the wall in the first place. In any event, my magic created a land bridge about two feet wide over the chasm. It told me the project was doable. I was getting ready to add to my bridge so it wouldn't fall in when something drilled into my magical center. Power poured from me. At first, I was certain I could stop it."

"Except you couldn't." Cyn's deep voice was oddly soothing.

"That's right. I tried everything. When nothing worked, I panicked for all the good it did me. I was stuck. Figured I'd be in that eerie cave for all eternity."

"I'd have tracked you down."

His assertion surprised me. "Why? I'm not one of your subjects."

"I care about you. Also, you were there because of me. Go on."

Before I got tangled up in him saying he cared about me, I forged ahead. "Things grew fuzzy after that, and I may have hallucinated the voice, but I begged for my freedom. A disembodied voice told me I had enough magic to heal the break. I told it I needed to pace myself, but whatever it was paid me no heed. Finally, the voice told me it would take care of me, and it called me *daughter of my bones.* Do you have any idea who I was talking to? Or what daughter of my bones means?"

Cynwrigg drew his fair brows together. Rather than answering me, he asked, "How'd you escape?"

"Not under my own steam. Once the gap was shut, something moved me back to my starting point. Turned out I had a wee bit of magic left, and it was actually expanding, which shouldn't have been happening. I sat there for a while trying to figure things out and then teleported to where I replenish my power."

I waited to see if he was going to address what I'd asked him. Midnight jumped into his lap purring up a storm, and he scratched the cat's ears. "You bear good news," he said at last.

"Yes, it's a plus the breach is healed," I agreed.

Cyn shook his head. "Nay, not that, although it's also welcome tidings. The voice would have to belong to Faery. She has a vested interest in her integrity. She's who stole your magic. Once she saw how well it worked, I can imagine her grabbing what she could to fix the problem."

He blew out a weary breath. "She created the rift to get my attention. It must have gotten out of hand because she wasn't able to close it on her own. She can't talk with me because Oberon bound her in some way. Apparently, she can talk with others, though. I'm delighted the old bastard didn't have enough power to totally muffle her."

I chewed my lower lip, thinking. "I figured it had to be her too, but it seemed too fantastic to be true."

"Meanwhile," he went on, "the dragons warned the court if we couldn't sever Oberon's bond with the land, Faery would die. Their seers have never been wrong that I know, so it's one more problem to address."

"Did the dragons sketch out a timeline?" I asked.

"Nay. Neither did I ask, which I should have. I got the impression it was an emergent problem, though, not one that would wait for a decade until someone got around to it."

I was still stuck on the daughter of my bones pronouncement. "Why would Faery label me daughter in any way? And why of her bones? What are her bones, anyway? The foundations of Faery?"

"I do not know."

An unexpected wave of disappointment washed through me, crested, and headed out to sea. I'd been both eager to understand and leery at the same time. If Cynwrigg didn't know, the unsolved riddle had to wait for another day—perhaps another time entirely. "What happened with the court?" I asked, relieved to move the topic away from myself.

He tilted the bottle of beer he'd been holding and took a deep swig from it. "It would be nice to say everyone jumped into their new roles as spies to flush out traitors, but most of the court shied away from turning in people—and animals—they've known all their lives."

Something about that didn't sit right. "Why?" I asked. "Do they want more innocents like Rona to die?"

"I've been considering...everything. Before I left, my cousin, Aedan, was starting to look like an enemy. To be on the safe side, I corralled him until I can return."

I gasped at the implications. "You're afraid the court is riddled with rogues?"

"Titania's tits, I hope not. Maybe one or two, but surely not all twelve of them."

Perhaps sensing Cyn's agitation, Midnight jumped from his lap to mine. "Nothing much better here, buddy," I told him and rubbed a special spot under his chin.

"Even if it's only one," I spoke slowly, "they'll alert all the bad apples."

"That didn't escape me." Cyn drained his beer and set the bottle on the floor with a thump.

"How can you determine who to trust?" I flapped a hand his way. "Never mind. Rhetorical question."

He raked curved fingers through his hair. "I have to return to Faery as soon as possible. I just made the rounds in the casino, and I told everyone I might be gone for a few days."

"Don't worry about helping me move. I'll figure it out. Rent is paid on both places, so there's no special hurry."

He angled a deeply speculative glance my way. I felt his power as it settled around my glamour, seeking a way inside.

"What are you doing?" I asked.

"It seems I'm forever asking things of you, but I want you to come back to Faery with me."

The chair and I were done. To make a bad pun in a gaming house, remaining still wasn't in the cards. Feet under me and cat on the floor, I said, "But that will be dangerous for you. I'm not welcome in Faery. Mother gave up everything, and—"

"If I have my way, I'll see her back within Faery's gates too," Cyn interrupted me. "I was tossing power about to break your glamour. I couldn't. If I can't drill through it, no one else in Faery can, either. So long as it's intact, you should be safe enough, but it's your choice."

"That librarian, Ysir, knew I was there."

"Aye, but not what you are. He was reacting to Witch magic in my rooms."

"Do you know that?" I demanded. "Have you spoken with him?"

"No, but others have. If he'd labeled you a hybrid, someone would have come running to me. That kind of news doesn't stay bottled up."

"Why?" I asked.

"Because everyone in Faery loves to gossip."

I shook my head. "Not what I meant. Why do you want me to come with you?"

He hesitated before answering. Not long, but enough time elapsed for me to add, "The real reason, and don't sugarcoat it. I'll know."

I expected him to focus on our mutual attraction. Undeniably strong, it had to be driving him as much as it did me. So far, I'd been successful dodging its pull, but not without difficulty.

He did no such thing. "This may sound odd," he said, "overdramatic, but my instincts are sound. I've always trusted them, and they're telling me we belong together through this conflict. That our magic is complementary. Faery obviously agrees. She wouldn't have siphoned your power if she didn't see it as a perfect match for her energies. Nor would she have labeled you daughter if there weren't truth to it."

I'd begun to pace as I digested his thoughts. Much as I wanted them to be true, they seemed like a flight of fancy. "You're looking for allies," I murmured. "For someone you know you can trust. It's not surprising—"

He held up a hand. "Not the case at all. I'll be the first to acknowledge I was a reluctant regent. The part about needing allies is correct, but I'm not so desperate I'll resort to making things up. Saying they're true to pretend they are." He stood. "I need to leave, Dariyah. Will you come with me or no?"

A sudden chill walked down my spine. I've never been much for prophecies, but I felt certain if I accepted my life would never, ever be the same. "Can I think about it?"

"Let's take an hour. We'll crack a few heads together and move what you want to your new place. At the end of that time, I'm leaving, and I hope you'll accompany me."

Insight hammered me. "You won't be returning to Earth, will you?"

"Depending on how things go, not permanently. I need to find a solid manager for the casino, but I could accomplish that in a couple of hours." He dropped his hands on my shoulders. "Faery is no longer a benign place. I might not survive, in which case the casino won't matter. You could be walking into danger even worse than what I face, if your dual nature is uncovered."

"Or not," I muttered.

"What do you mean?"

"Faery seems to believe I'm part of her. She saved me once. I don't imagine she'll stand back while someone slaughters me." I left it there.

"Maybe you're onto something I hadn't taken into consideration. I assumed she'd marked you because she viewed you as a Witch, but I could be seriously off base about that. Shall we leave Midnight here until we're done with the moving project?"

"Nah. Let's take him. I'll set him loose him in the old place until the dust settles."

Cyn nodded. The familiar feel of his power swathed me in a teleport spell. I'd almost decided to go with him, but I'd keep my mouth shut until I was certain. I'd assumed the pull of Faery was so strong because of my Fae blood, but I was beginning to suspect it ran far deeper than that.

Mother had known. She knew everything. Too bad there wasn't time to pay her a visit and tell her it was long past time to reveal the whole shebang. Gloves off. No more secrets. They'd served a purpose, but their day was done, and they'd turned into stumbling blocks. Impediments that might mean the difference between Faery's survival or her demise.

CHAPTER TWELVE, CYN

Dispatching Oberon's minions had been quick and almost fun. A shifter, a Witch, and a Fae, they'd gone down like bowling pins in an arcane alley. Midnight disappeared as soon as he hit his familiar turf, and Dariyah sorted the few belongings she wanted to transport, dropping them in a central location in her single room. Clothes, cooking implements, and electronics made a messy pile.

"No furniture?" I raised an eyebrow.

"Nope. I'll buy new. The apartment is a whole lot bigger than this flat, so I'd need stuff anyway."

I eyed the growing pile until she stood over it and said, "There. That should do it. What do you think?"

"Two choices. We can construct a container and move everything in one batch."

"Or?" She arched her red brows.

"Several trips with what we can carry. The container will take a few minutes to put together, but will save time in the end."

"Show me. It's not magic I'm familiar with."

I mixed earth and air into a bombproof weave around her possessions. Once it was complete, I told it to shrink everything. We ended up with a good-sized carton. A smile formed on her full lips. "Wow. Neat trick." She bent to lift one end. I got the other.

The scent of her magic wafted around me, heady as a fine, old wine. When it cleared we stood in a large, empty room. "You weren't exaggerating about this being larger than your last place," I commented.

"Beggars can't be choosers," she said. "I needed something fast, and this was available. It's more space than I require, but at least I won't have to watch my back every minute I'm outside. This is a better neighborhood."

"I know. I bought a place not far from here, except I never spend any time there." I spoke a few words, and the container expanded to its original size and vanished; its contents spilled onto the pale-beige rug. The moment had come, and I faced it squarely. "Are you coming to Faery?"

"I am."

A blast of pure joy raced through me, but I felt

selfish—and worried. What if something happened? What if my pretty words about our magic being additive were nothing beyond wishful thinking? "I'll do my best to protect you," I said, and meant it.

She shook her head. "You will do no such thing. I'm capable of caring for myself. If you split your attention too many ways, it might not go well." Walking to me, she nested her head in the hollow between my neck and shoulder. "We'll take care of each other."

Her remark touched me in a way nothing else had, maybe ever. Because I lacked words to convey the warmth fluttering through me, I said, "I like that idea." To cover my discomfiture, I drew a travel spell together and loosed it. Moments later, the walls of my chamber in Dubrova castle formed around us.

My rooms were empty save Aedan still wrapped in his cage of doom. He'd sunk into a crouch, arms around his knees and wasn't moving, an improvement over yelling and ripping his hair out as he cursed me.

I felt a small ripple as Dariyah strengthened her glamour. Good woman. She pointed at the cage. "I assume that's your cousin. The one you can't trust."

Her extended hand caught Aedan's attention. He shot to his feet, mouth moving, but nothing leaked through my sound shield. I didn't want to hear him spew poison, anyway. "Aye, it is," I replied.

"What are you going to do with him?" She settled

her hands on her hips as she transited Aedan's impromptu prison.

"Good question. I suppose I can leave him here. The cage will hold him nicely."

"I have a better idea. *Feed him to Faery. See what she thinks.*" Dariyah had switched to telepathy, but I was fairly certain the sound shield cut both ways.

"He can't hear us. If we do that, it will place him where Oberon can free him," I told her.

"Are you positive Aedan's on his payroll?"

"Not 100 percent, no," I admitted.

She shrugged. "Maybe because Faery treated fairly with me, I trust her. I was vulnerable. She could have stripped me of power and gone on her merry way. She didn't. Oberon may have stolen her capacity to talk with you, but she appears otherwise intact."

Dariyah's mouth rounded into an O. I recognized that expression. "You thought of something else, didn't you?"

"I did, indeed. Let me dig through his mind, see what I come up with. And then we'll feed him to Faery." She drew her brows into a thin line. "If he's part of the rebellion—or whatever you want to call it—he could help us track down the others."

"And with a whole lot less effort than knocking on doors," I agreed. "I have to free him, first, though."

"Too much magic in the cage to drill through?"

I nodded, but she walked around it again, anyway, jabbing its weave with her brand of power. "Damn it. I'd hoped I could find a way through. I can, but it won't leave me with enough juice to do much else."

"We'll need to be quick," I cautioned. "First thing crybaby will do is use telepathy to summon Oberon. The next will be trying to teleport out of here. I can short-circuit that part and hold him in place for as long as you require."

"I won't need much time. Stripping minds of information is one of my specialties." Her smile was cool and vicious. It was the side of her I'd seen in the casino when I made her free the dealer from the trance she'd imposed. Or maybe I hadn't made her do anything. If she hadn't wanted to let him go, she'd have destroyed his puny mind. All her years alone had honed solid survival skills.

Another idea pushed to center stage. "I'm not sure I can finesse this, but the cage is already built, and—"

"Yes!" She nodded enthusiastically. "Drop it back over his head as soon as I'm done, and then move him out of here and let Faery take over. Mother raised me on tales of sacrifices to Faery. The best use for that one"— she hooked a finger at Aedan—"is to strengthen the land. She'll absorb his magic and cast the husk aside."

I'd heard those legends too, and discounted them as tales to keep errant children in line. I should have paid closer attention. Gathering power, I let it build to make certain I'd maximize our probability of success. On the far side of the cage, Dariyah was doing the same. Clearly intuiting we had something unpleasant in store for him, Aedan was beating the sides of the enclosure with his fists. Blood ran down his knuckles and the enchanted wall circling him.

"Tell me when you're ready," I told Dariyah.

"Almost. Okay. Now."

In one fell swoop, I jerked the cage upward, taking care to maintain its integrity. Aedan looked dazed. It took him at least a count of ten to understand he was free. Dariyah had long since latched on to his thoughts. I was ready for him to make a dash for freedom as he screamed for Oberon in telepathy that was probably audible for half a kilometer.

I'd expected a teleport spell, but his magic was weak, and he was too shaken to execute anything quite so complex. He lurched toward the door. I jumped on him and pushed him to the thick carpet covering my floor. I'd presumed he'd land a few punches, at least attempt to fight back, but his warrior skills were as lacking as his magic.

No wonder he clung to Oberon. If anyone needed a protector, it was the weak suck, poor excuse for a mage, sprawled beneath my bulk. I dragged one arm behind him, holding it a couple of degrees from breaking. My other arm was hooked around his neck, bending it back as I straddled his ass.

A shiny nimbus surrounded his head reflecting blues and violets. In the middle of all that color, a stream of light flowed from him to Dariyah's outstretched hands. Her face was twisted into a harsh expression, and she rocked back on her heels as if the sheer volume of information were daunting. As abruptly as her power had flared, she withdrew it.

"All done." She was panting but reached for the cage suspended a meter in the air above Aedan's head.

"Let me go. Please." Aedan's voice sounded rusty, as if he hadn't used it in ages.

"Please, huh? We'll let Faery decide what to do with you." I released his throat, but kept his arm bent at an unnatural angle as I dragged him to his feet.

He stared at Dariyah. "What are you? No Witch alive could do what you just did."

She stared back. "Eh, we're more powerful than most think. It's one of those well-kept secrets" Reaching upward, she hooked the lower edge of the cage with her fingertips.

"Noooooo." A long, low moan dribbled from Aedan. "Faery will kill me."

"So will Oberon," I informed my cousin tartly. "He used you and however many others—"

"Lots," Dariyah cut in. "So many, it's hard to fathom."

The statement alarmed me. I'd figured there were a bare handful of conspirators at most. I'd deal with the list later. I had a message to impart to Aedan, one I hoped he'd pass up his skanky ranks if he escaped Faery's clutches. "Oberon's vision was always to limit Faery to the Fae. How in the hell he conscripted non-Fae to implement his plan is beyond me, but you're done here. How many others on the court are corrupt?"

"She knows," Aedan replied dully. "Ask her."

"She'll know names, not where they fit into Faery. I'm asking you." I gave his arm a shake. The bone must have been holding on by a few cells because I heard it break, followed by a piteous shriek from Aedan.

"For the love of the goddess, man up," I gritted. "Who else on the court is a rogue operator?"

"All the Fae but Jess," he moaned.

I felt his pathetic attempt to muster healing magic. He'd never been this inept, so I asked, "Why are you so weak?"

"Oberon has been feeding off them all," Dariyah answered and dropped the cage into place.

Breath banged through my teeth as I stared at a man I'd called both friend and kinsman. How could I have been so deluded?

"We see what we want to see," Dariyah said softly.

"And what we expect is there," I added. "He and I were young together. We—" I sliced a hand downward to distance myself from reminiscing about our idyllic youth. Whatever Aedan and I had been to one another, it was long dead. He'd known, probably for a very long time. Of the two of us, I was the slow learner.

He was done pounding on the cage. Looking at him standing with slumped shoulders, arm hanging at an awkward angle, I felt sorry for him. He'd bet on the wrong horse, and it had been his undoing.

Dariyah walked to my side and placed a hand on my arm. "How are you doing? He was your kinsman."

Her words drew me out of my musings. "Aedan fucked up. I have no business romanticizing his actions. And he sure as hell doesn't deserve my pity." Linking to the magic powering the cage, I sent it downward to the subterranean underpinnings of Faery. She could take things from here.

If Oberon intercepted her and freed Aedan, I'd deal with it later.

"Open your mind," Dariyah said. "Most of what I dredged out of him doesn't make a whole lot of sense to me, but it will to you."

By the time she was done transferring information, my view of Faery had taken a definite downward turn.

"Cynwrigg?" Her voice was gentle, and she tightened her grip on my arm.

"Aye. Earth is looking better by the moment, but not until I clean up this mess."

"It's so many," she said. "I wanted to stop emptying his mind long before I was done."

"The hardest part for me," I told her, "is recognizing the extent of bigotry riddling Faery. We've always looked down our noses at mages not native to our land."

"Like Witches," she said dryly.

I nodded. "Exactly like that. Shifters too. It was wrong. I always knew as much, but I never lifted a finger to stop the dark jokes about mages we considered inferior. I'm not sure when the poison spread to anyone who wasn't Fae."

"Can't go back," she said and added, "Could you have tapped into his mind?"

"Yes, but not as quickly or efficiently as you did." I considered the implications of what I'd just found out. "The court just became worthless."

"Not worthless. It needs new delegates, though."

"Seems like a low priority. For now, I won't call it into session. Better no court than one riddled by blackguards and rogues."

"Does it hold regular meetings?" She glanced up, catching my gaze with hers.

"Sure, around the four major festivals. The next one coming up is Lughnasa, but it's not for a few weeks."

"Good to have time." She let go of me and added, "What's next?"

Bitter laughter wanted out. I kept it contained. "Looking for strangers fomenting riots in Faery misses the point. My bet is one of the people on that horrendously long list was behind the unicorn's slaughter."

"Speaking of the list, who's represented on it? Are all of them Fae?"

"You'd think they should be, but they aren't. No animals, but plenty of Fae and Sidhe."

"What will you do to them?"

I'd been thinking about it because I had to do something. Not knowing and not doing was one thing. The bitch about knowledge is it requires action. I unclenched my jaw. "I'd like to end every single one of them. Permanently. Except it isn't practical."

"Word will get out." Dariyah nodded. "People will flee, which isn't a bad thing, except some of them will continue to create problems, and Faery will stop being a haven."

"Newsflash," I noted sourly. "Sanctuary departed long ago."

She closed her teeth over her lower lip. "It didn't seem that way to me. When I first came here to these rooms, I felt wanted and welcome. Don't make this worse than it is."

"As in, with all this shit, there has to be a pony somewhere?" A corner of my mouth twitched, but smiling wasn't happening. Aedan's reluctant revelation had ripped the moorings out from under me.

"Exactly. Look for ponies. It's how I've survived."

"I've changed my mind. I'm starting with the court," I said. "I'm going to call an emergency meeting."

"I'm confused. I thought you wanted to steer clear of it."

"I wasn't thinking. The others who sit on the court take their duties seriously. I will interrogate the guilty ones and let the rest of the delegates vote on appropriate action."

"It won't be easy to prove their complicity," Dariyah warned.

"Might be simpler than you assume. Truth spells have their uses. Particularly once I lead out with what we did to Aedan."

"I will be there, but warded. No reason to reveal myself unless something unexpected happens."

I placed an arm around her shoulders and squeezed before letting go. She'd just saved me an awkward moment. I wanted her by my side. She belonged there, but if she stood next to me, the focus would fall on her, not on the treachery I was committed to uncovering.

Witches in Faery weren't unheard of, but one had never been included in a court event. It was part of the problem, of the xenophobia turning Faery rotten to her roots.

Now that my eyes had been pried open, I understood the dilemma all too clearly. Faery provided a refuge for all mages, regardless of persuasion. It was how she'd been designed. Oberon had accepted the precept for many years. I couldn't pin down when he'd changed, but he had.

"Oberon wasn't always a dick?" A corner of Dariyah's mouth turned downward.

I did smile then. "Guess I need to get used to you being in my head."

She gave an awkward little shrug. "Sorry. Old habits and all that."

"It's all right."

"Truly?"

I nodded, but didn't add how much I welcomed her nearness. Like as not, she already knew. "Oberon always had dickish tendencies, but he used to be fair. We'd joke about Titania keeping him on track."

"But she's gone, right?"

"Right. Welcome to problem number three hundred."

"It's not as bad as all that. We'll knock 'em down one at a time."

As far as I looked, all I saw was conflict stretching around me, but I'd moved from making excuses to a let's-kick-some-ass mindset. Raising my mind voice, I pinged the eleven court delegates and told them to drop whatever they were engaged in and hustle to the courtroom. I had important news about the vigilantes, news that wouldn't wait.

CHAPTER THIRTEEN, DARIYAH

My heart went out to Cyn, and for the first time I understood the advantages of not having friends or family. Being a loner meant no one disappointed me. I'd seen the pain in his eyes at his cousin's betrayal. Recognized when he'd pulled himself back from the brink of falling into looking backward and reliving all the good times they'd shared.

My solitary existence offered cold comfort, but it wasn't as if I'd had a choice. I stood behind Cynwrigg's seat in the courtroom, leaning against the wall. My ward should be bulletproof, but I tested it for the fourth time, making sure no chinks of power bled through.

An interesting assortment of mages and animals ranged around the long table. I was grouping satyrs with animals, but they probably considered themselves more man than goat. The Sidhe had gorgeous fluttery wings. I'd always been slightly disappointed mine had never grown. I'd had small buds in the center of my back, but they'd never turned into anything. Perhaps because they'd been vestigial, they'd withered and dropped away before I hit my twentieth year.

The court chamber was impressive. A high coved ceiling inset with stained glass depicted a leaping unicorn. Silken wall hangings showed every variety of magical person and beast working side by side. If Oberon had his way, all the artwork would have to go, replaced by Fae-only pieces.

What had happened to wed him to hegemony? Power corrupts, but surely he could see the value in mixed magics. Even I, outlier that I was, understood differing types of power shored one another up.

It was the bedrock of my own ability.

Cyn remained standing as the court hurried in. What he'd told them lit a fire under both innocent and guilty. I took a moment to examine the Fae. Which one was Jess? Had he—or maybe she—been offered a piece of the pie and declined? While it was better than accepting, it still made him complicit in a plot he should have taken straight to Cynwrigg.

Eh, I shouldn't be so quick to condemn. Maybe the game plan involved feeling people out. If they didn't bite on the first offer, which didn't reveal much, they remained clueless. The more I rolled it around, the likelier it seemed. No one plopped their entire hand on the table right off the bat.

"Thank you for assembling so quickly," Cyn was saying. "I value and appreciate your support."

It could have been my imagination, but the Fae, sitting grouped together on the right side, seemed to squirm a little. No clues there about who Jess might be.

"What did you discover, Regent?" The unicorn craned his neck toward Cyn.

"A number of things," he replied smoothly. "Let's start with an expansion of what I told you before about Oberon setting spies to watch me on Earth."

A chorus of displeasure ran through the room, peppered with, "That's horrid," and "How could he?" One of the Fae shouted. "That's not new, though. You demanded this meeting because you had new information."

"The way I found out," Cyn went on, ignoring the Fae, "is I apprehended the most recent hire. She was quite candid. No reason not to be. All she was was contract labor. By then, Oberon had fired her." He blew out a breath. "Apparently, he's done this before and developed quite the reputation for being a shyster. He hires mages from a central registry I had no idea existed, collects information on me for a while, and then presents the mage du jour with a deal. They're to go away quietly for half the agreed upon sum. If they make a stink about it, they get nothing."

Stamping hoofs suggested the satyrs and unicorn weren't surprised. "Very like the old charlatan," a satyr spoke up.

"Aye, and he cheats at dice too," the other one muttered.

"It is well within his character, isn't it?" Cyn had never bothered to take his seat. He raised his fair brows as he let his gaze settle on one court member after another. "The next bit of information I ferreted out is that Oberon has muffled Faery so she cannot speak with me. The rift, which is cured, was her way of flagging my attention."

Where before a buzz of conversation had rippled through the chamber, it fell by the wayside. Silence reigned.

"How'd you fix the rift?" a Fae asked.

"Aye, we'd all like to know. And where is Aedan," another chimed in.

"Aedan is a traitor. Unless Oberon horned in and freed him, he is with Faery, who will serve as judge and jury for his sins." Cyn's voice was flat. His multihued gaze bored into the Fae who'd asked. He'd led out with information about me, something they already knew, to offer a false sense of security, but it was well on its way out.

"How'd you come to that conclusion," the Fae shot back.

"I tapped into his mind."

The Fae looked away, studying something on the wall above my head.

"What did you find there, in Aedan's mind?" the unicorn whinnied.

"We have been set upon from within," Cyn told the court. "No one new has infiltrated Faery. Oberon couldn't promulgate his Fae-only vision from inside our lands because over half our population isn't Fae, so he chose to work another angle."

"That's a cheap shot," one of the Fae shouted.

"Aye," another broke in. "You're making unfounded assumptions. Most of us are extremely openminded."

"Do tell," Cyn went on smoothly. "Assumptions or no, I believe it's why Oberon left. Our human visitors may have hastened his egress, but ever since he left, he's been inciting discontent to forward his vision of a land open only to Fae."

"Fuck him," a satyr snorted. "He tried to do the same when he was still here, but never managed to gain much leverage."

Cyn had just said exactly the same thing. He raised

his hands. Power flowed from them, heading right for the group of seated Fae. "Approach me," he ordered.

Because they hadn't anticipated he'd snare them in a spell, they lacked warding. Powerless against Cyn's injunction, they stumbled to their feet and walked toward him, standing in two lines. He added a truth net to compulsion and boomed, "One at a time. When did you pledge fealty to Oberon once he absented himself as monarch?"

A woman in the back row tossed white hair behind her shoulders. "I turned him down."

"Why didn't you tell me?" Cyn skewered her with his implacable gaze.

"I thought about it, but it didn't seem important." She exhaled noisily. "Faery is a peaceful place. I figured even if Oberon were making an end run, he'd fail because he wasn't here. Most of my time is spent next to the rivers gathering stones and making charms and jewelry." She bowed her head. "I failed you, Regent. For that, I am truly sorry."

"Return to your seat, Jess," he told her.

Once she'd left, he turned to the others. "I'm waiting."

"We owe you nothing." A Fae with cropped black hair rolled his shoulders back.

Something changed in Cynwrigg. It was like a shell cracking open so something grander could emerge. He narrowed his eyes. "Wrong. You owe me fealty. I am your named regent. As such, I am the living representative of the land you inhabit."

The man next to the dark-haired Fae sneered and turned his grey eyes on Cyn. "We remain loyal to Oberon. He is the one linked to Faery. The day is rapidly approaching when he will return and take up his rightful place."

"Shut up," another Fae hissed.

"Why?" the grey-eyed one countered. "It's no longer a secret. Pretty-boy up there"—he jerked his chin at Cyn—"finally figured shit out. Took him a while."

"Not as dumb as you thought I was, eh?" Anger ran hot beneath Cyn's words. I didn't blame him.

A flash of motion was my only warning before the unicorn executed a stunning leap over the table and cantered the length of the room, stopping behind the small group of Fae. "Which of you cast the magic to kill my Rona?" he roared.

"Stand down," Cynwrigg bellowed.

"No. This is my battle. And it's personal." The unicorn didn't even spare Cyn a passing glance. He jabbed his horn into the nearest Fae back. "Answer me, or I shall kill you all and take joy from it. Nothing can bring Rona back, but the penalty for killing one of my herd is death."

Cyn tightened the weave of both truth and compulsion spells. "Answer him. It won't bother me a whit to turn the lot of you over to the land once he's finished. She can suck the magic from your bones and spit what's left into the void."

The remaining mages had closed ranks, moving forward and forming a ragged circle around the doomed Fae. What a shit-show. I'd felt bad for Mother, sorry she'd been forced into exile, but if this pathetic bunch of fucks would have been my kinsmen, I was revising my opinion fast.

With a great show of it-was-hims and he-did-its, sorting truth from fiction was simple. Cyn's truth net only pinged sweetly for the first Fae to speak. Besides, he was the one doing major finger-pointing at the others.

"With your leave, Regent." The unicorn's horn was jammed against the dark-haired Fae's back right between his shoulder blades.

"Noooo. You're making a mistake," the Fae moaned. "I've been working for you, Cynwrigg, the whole time. A double agent. Aye, that's it."

"Nice try since this is the first I've heard about your extraordinary loyalty," Cyn mocked and nodded at the unicorn.

Death by unicorn isn't pretty, but legends hadn't prepared me for the swiftness of the golden horn. It mowed through the Fae's body as if there was no internal resistance at all. When it emerged, organs dangled from its tip. With an up-and-down motion, the unicorn shucked whatever had been on his horn, drew back, and pushed more of the Fae's innards onto the floor. When unicorns killed, they sucked souls in the wake of their carnage. It ensured even the most hardy of immortals remained dead.

How was the Fae still on his feet? The horn. It had to be the only thing holding the dead-Fae-walking upright. My attention had been fixed on him. I didn't notice the other four link their magic until the air around them developed a characteristic blur that screamed teleport spell.

No time to alert Cyn. By the time I did that, the guilty Fae would be long gone. My actions could cost me everything—but only if someone pierced my glamour. Power jetted from my hands as my ward crumpled to the floor. "Stop them," I shouted and swathed layer upon layer of power around the Fae to unseat their spell.

"Who are you?" A satyr added magic to mine.

"A friend," Cyn shouted at him and added power to the mix. His move might have been instinctive, but I was blown away by how strong we were together. We'd never actually married our skills before. The vortex I'd put in place around the Fae turned from a nip-and-tuck proposition to a barrier that could last the ages. Not that it needed to.

"Kill them all," Cyn ordered, his tone flat, devoid of emotion.

"With pleasure." The unicorn gored another, and then another. "This is for your part in Rona's death," he repeated with each thrust. The coppery bite of blood filled the chamber, along with the stench of spilled entrails. Despite the grisly scene playing out before me, the feel of my magic slotted with Cyn's was heady.

Like nothing I'd ever felt before, our power was born to be joined. The rightness of it was like a shot between the eyes. Did he feel it too? I had no idea.

"What manner of Witch holds your level of magic?" the satyr who'd asked who I was challenged me.

The unicorn had the traitors well in hand. Too bad this batch wouldn't spell an end to the unrest in Faery, except I knew better. I exchanged a glance with Cynwrigg and dismantled my portion of what had turned into a joint spell. Turning to face the satyr, I said, "One who's taken care to study." I stuck out a hand. "Dari here."

The satyr aimed his next words at Cyn. "She's the mage for hire you intercepted." It wasn't a question. I had to hand it to him, he was sharp. I'd never known any satyrs before, but if they were all like this one, they were a shrewd lot.

"She is," Cyn agreed. "And kind enough to offer her

continued assistance because there's no love lost between her and Oberon."

The unicorn stood over the last Fae, flanks heaving and his golden horn covered in blood. He tossed his head back, full mane flying off to one side. "Thank you, Regent. Their deaths will not restore my Rona, but I have avenged her passing."

"Give me a moment," Cyn told the group ranged around the dead Fae. No one had said anything, except for the satyr. Their faces wore grim expressions as they regarded men they'd probably known for centuries, men who'd turned against everything Faery held dear.

I wanted to say something comforting, but I was an outsider. Nothing I said would mean anything since they'd assume I couldn't fathom the depth of their loss. It wasn't so much the dead traitors, but a loss of innocence, of belief in the inherent goodness in their fellows. Both had sustained a blow as fatal as the unicorn's gorings.

Loss of innocence was where I lived. If I'd ever had any, it had been snatched from me not long after I'd been born. Cyn motioned to me and I moved to his side. "Work with me," he said. "We are transporting the bodies to Faery."

For the second time in the last half hour, his power clicked into place, riding alongside mine and yielding the same intoxicating rush. He set the coordinates for transport; I packaged the not-quite-corpses. Life still flickered in one Fae. I felt certain Faery would snuff it out. The land had sounded desolate and furious about Oberon's betrayal when she'd spoken to me.

Cyn chanted a few words; the bodies broke apart into motes of blackness before they vanished leaving pools of blood on the wooden floor and nearest rug. A few more words from Cynwrigg in a form of Gaelic so old I wasn't familiar with it, and the blood lifted, forming droplets that were absorbed into the weave of air flowing through the chamber.

"In the end, their blood and bones and magic will strengthen our home," Cyn intoned and dropped his hands to his sides. My link to him snuffed out, leaving me aching for more.

"We must fill the court," the unicorn said.

"We will solicit delegates and hold an election," one of the Sidhe said. Her wings drooped, and she sounded shaken.

"I volunteer to go house to house, all through our lands," Jess said in a choked voice. "If I hadn't been so certain Oberon's offer was ridiculous, much of this might have been averted."

"How long ago did he come to you?" Cyn asked.

Jess narrowed her eyes in thought. "At least eighty years, perhaps a bit more."

"Interesting," Cyn mused. "Oberon's perfidy began not long after he left Faery."

"The Fae who sat on the court can't be the only ones he co-opted to his cause," I pointed out. I didn't want to draw attention to myself, but it was an important point, one that shouldn't get lost.

"We vote in new delegates every two years," Cyn pointed out. "Lots of chances for rogues to line the court chamber."

"Perhaps all his allies aren't Fae," the unicorn replied. He seemed to have caught his breath, and the blood on his horn had vanished. He angled the horn my way. "For example, you're a Witch. Oberon didn't have any compunctions about hiring you."

"Scuttlebutt at the registry was he'd hire anyone willing to take on the work," I said. "The rumor mill also said he wasn't honest, but I needed a job at the time."

"Glad to make your acquaintance, Dari," the unicorn whinnied.

"You as well," I told him, touched by his ready acceptance of me.

Two Sidhe fluttered closer to me, their jewel-toned wings quivering. "Be welcome, my dear," the fairy with violet hair said.

"Indeed," the other chimed in. "Faery has always been a retreat, a place of peace for all with magic." She aimed a sour look Cyn's way. "Not only Fae."

He bowed low. "I know it well. Oberon gave up trying to convince me Fae were superior to other mages a couple of centuries ago. Mostly because I changed the subject every time he brought it up."

He raised his hands, palms out. The murmur of voices quieted. "Thank you for everything," he told the delegates. "The story of the Fae who perished in this hall must be heard throughout the land. I agree with Dariyah about this batch being the tip of an iceberg." He paused to take a measured breath. "I was asked what I found in Aedan's mind. I have a list of everyone implicated in Oberon's nefarious scheme. There are a lot of them, and we must proceed with caution so as not to alarm everyone else."

His nostrils flared. "Some of you may not agree with me, but if any traitors wish to leave, rather than continue living in a land that doesn't honor their bigotry, they can have a one-way ticket out of Faery.

"Three immediate tasks lie ahead." He extended a hand and counted off on his fingers. "One. Flushing out the other traitors. Two. Voting on delegates to fill our court and seating them as quickly as possible. Three. Finding Titania."

"How can we be positive new delegates won't be as corrupt as the Fae we dispatched?" a Sidhe asked.

"Even though I have a list, the long and short of it is we can't know for certain," Cyn answered. "Aedan's information may have had holes in it. If I were Oberon, I wouldn't have trusted him with much of anything."

"We will ask the goddess and the land for their blessing," a Sidhe said.

"Might not do any good if we can't keep Oberon out," the unicorn neighed raucously. "Not if he's been sneaking in to keep tabs on everything. He might have been able to hire out watching Cynwrigg, but I'd bet my horn he's been here checking on the land."

"My suspicion as well," I said. It earned me an approving mane-shake.

"I'm adding a fourth task," Cyn said. "Not keeping Oberon out, but building a series of markers that will alert us when he's here. If we intercept him enough times and make his life miserable enough—"

"What if he waltzes in and demands you return sovereignty to him?" a Sidhe asked. "It would be within our covenant and his rights as king. It's not as if he stepped down."

I glanced at Cyn and received a curt nod, verifying the Sidhe's assertion. "He didn't step down," Cyn confirmed. "Just walked away. Twenty years slid past before I stopped expecting him back. Once the court is full, we will rewrite the covenant."

"Why wait?" the Sidhe demanded.

"To make certain he can't challenge our action. We will also have the covenant ratified by Faery assuming I can figure out a way to include her. We all have work to do."

Amid a sea of nodding heads, the unicorn, satyrs, Jess, and the Sidhe strode from the courtroom leaving me alone with Cynwrigg. Tucking a hand beneath his arm, I asked, "How are you doing?"

"Surprisingly well, given how bloody this turned."

"What were you expecting?"

"That I'd kill whoever was responsible for Rona's death myself and let the others leave with the understanding they could never return." He turned me until I faced him. "This way was better. More permanent."

"Were you certain Rona's assassin sat on the court?"

He shook his head. "What I was certain of was the group on the court would know who'd masterminded her death." The harsh cast to his mouth softened. "At least I was right about one thing."

I had a feeling what he was about to say, but I asked anyway. "And what was that?"

"Our magics. When they're joined, it's like nothing I've ever experienced." He cradled the side of my face in his big hand. "You felt it, right? The jolt as our power collided."

I nodded, my mouth curving into a soft smile. "How could I not feel it? It was like a tidal wave, a tsunami of magic."

"We need to practice, of course." He smiled back, so maybe my grin was infectious.

"You sound like my mother. On a serious note, there's work to be done."

"There is. We're starting with Faery. But first, I hope you don't mind me taking credit for you scouring Aedan's memories."

"Not at all. It would have been awkward to say I'd done it. Make it that much harder to keep up my pretense of being a Witch."

"Thanks for understanding. Let's pay Faery a visit."

It wouldn't have been my first choice of a launching point. I'd figured we'd use our combined strength to search out other traitors. "Why there?"

"Because she can talk to you. It's a workaround for Oberon muting her ability to speak with me." He hesitated. "I understand if you have other things to do. We can schedule Faery for a time that's more convenient."

I threaded my arms around him. "When I committed to do whatever it took to bring Oberon down, I meant it. Let's go chat with Faery. Maybe after that, we can grab something to eat."

Muted rumbling shook the castle. "Fuck!" Cyn swore as his power boiled around us. "Last time I felt something like that was when you closed the rift."

"Oberon couldn't have ripped it open again," I

protested, wanting desperately to believe my own hype. I liked Faery; she deserved respect not destruction.

"Yeah, he could have. He'll have discovered the deaths of his pets, and he'll be furious, bent on revenge."

I dragged my power to the fore, ready for anything as Cyn's spell transported us to the bowels of his world. Mine too, except I wasn't used to thinking in those terms.

❧ 14 ❧

CHAPTER FOURTEEN, CYN

If I ever got my hands on Oberon, I wouldn't let go until I'd made him sorry he'd ever fucked with me. Anger wasn't useful; it clouded my reason, but I wanted Oberon tossed in a pit, hacked at with knives, frozen until his balls turned blue, and burned to a crisp. Preferably all at the same time with me presiding over the festivities.

A cyclone whooshed through Faery's underground lair tossing up not only dirt but fist-sized rocks in its wake. "What the hell?" Dariyah cried, but her next words were ripped away by the wind.

I tried to shield her with my body; she defeated my efforts and hurled magic around us both. It helped a little, but I couldn't see well enough to make out what was happening. Switching to my third eye finally pierced

227

the gray murk. Boulders had fallen from above; some perched precariously, lever and fulcrum poised to rain destruction on anyone in their path.

Power sheeted from me as I used it in lieu of eyes and ears. It was so loud from the *thwack* of rockfall, I couldn't hear a thing beyond the crash and crunch of boulders smashing into one another. The earth bucked and heaved under our feet.

"Faery must be under attack. This is her way of fighting back," I shouted.

"Let's help her!" Light crackled from Dariyah's fingertips.

I couldn't even find Aedan and the others I'd banished to this spot, let alone anyone else. "Love your enthusiasm, but do you see anyone to wrestle?"

"No, but Faery can't have launched all this for nothing," Dariyah pointed out.

"I sent Aedan and the other Fae here," I reminded her. "It might have sparked some kind of chain reaction."

"But they were already well on their way to being dead."

The storm swirling around us did seem like overkill. I reached for Faery with my mind and ran into the same dead end I always did. "Ask Faery." I nudged Dariyah.

She turned her green-eyed gaze my way. If we hadn't been standing next to one another, she'd have been tough to see with all the debris in the air. "I already did. Let me try again."

I swept us out of the path of a tumbling boulder. Dariyah's shielding would probably have stopped it, but why waste magic if we didn't have to?

Balancing power in one hand, she grabbed my arm with the other. "She answered me! Lower. We have to go lower. I'll take us."

Protests lodged in my throat and died there. This was my land. It rankled that Oberon had hamstrung me. Pushing my jumble of emotions aside—they'd only get in the way—I added my power to Dariyah's as we traveled through a psychedelic light show in blues and greens and reds. I expected another cavern, but we emerged in daylight on a grassy verge. Dotted with odd, stunted trees, a verdant plain stretched in every direction.

After the racket above, I welcomed silence, gentle breezes, and a cerulean sky sprinkled with fluffy clouds. What was this place?

Dariyah let go of my arm and spun until she faced me, but something had changed. She didn't feel the same. Worried something unspeakable had happened, I pushed magic toward her, seeking answers, but she shook her head.

"I am no longer myself in this place. I ceded my will to enable Faery to speak through me."

I curled my hands into fists. "Do not hurt Dariyah.

She is dear to me. After I leave here, I will find Oberon. When I do, I will kill him."

"I shall not harm her. You and she were destined to come together. You must leave Oberon alone for now. So long as he and I are linked, killing him will spell the end of Faery. Not immediately, but I will wither and die." Even her voice was different. No longer Dariyah's smooth, rich contralto, but something higher, sweeter, more like East Indian flutes.

"The unrest you stepped into above," she went on, "sprang from two things. Oberon came to claim his dead. I told him no. When he refused to honor my position, I stood in his way."

"Is he still there?" My question held dangerous edges, and Faery knew it.

She shook her head. "I buried his minions beneath tons of rock because I was curious how much they meant to him. He possessed sufficient magic to uncover them, but decided it was too much trouble. The dead are no longer of any use to him."

"Then why show up at all?" I asked.

"He was furious and had moved well beyond reason. He cannot stand to be bested, and I'd won this round. All of us did, but I was the final repository. It was me who dispensed justice for treason. My sentence included being barred from the *Dreaming* and separated from their immortal souls, elements that will continue even after their bodies cease to draw breath."

I spun my hands in a circle. "So he showed up, pitched a fit, and left when he didn't get his way."

Faery nodded sadly. The corners of her eyes drooped. "Being tethered to that horrible excuse for a king has been the bane of my existence."

A jab of insight made me ask, "Do you know where Titania is?"

"Of course. She's a prisoner on a distant world."

"How? Did he do something to her magic?"

She shook her head. "Nay, her mind. He wove webs around it, thick and confusing. She has moments of lucidity, but when she can't figure out where she is, she sinks back into a long sleep."

"I thought he loved her." It wasn't just me who believed that. Oberon and Titania's longstanding romance was the stuff of fables. Of course, their quarrels were as well.

"He may have, but he loves power more." Faery tossed her head back. "I must go. If I remain longer, I will damage my vessel, and I like her too much to do her harm."

"One more question?"

"Nay, no more time." The weave of air around Dariyah turned violet with silver threads running through it. When they cleared, she rocked from foot to foot, looking dazed.

I wrapped my arms around her. "Are you all right?"

"Yeah. My head hurts, but otherwise I'm fine. I heard all that. You should have asked her where Titania is."

"You're right. I should have, but you can ask for me."

Dariyah shook her head. "I can't. She's gone."

I stroked locks of red hair out of her face and rubbed the back of her neck. "Not that many 'distant worlds.' We'll stop by the library. Ysir is a genius when it comes to geography."

"He'll remember me."

"Probably not. He never actually laid eyes on you." Still holding her close, I set a spell in motion to take us to Faery's library. We'd won this sequence, but our victory would push Oberon to move his timetable up.

"He's bound to make mistakes," Dariyah said. "Especially, if he hurries."

"Still linked to my mind, eh?"

She offered a sunny smile. "It's so instructive."

Dusty shelves shaped up around us. Dariyah still looked a little peaked. "Are you sure you're all right?"

"Yes. Faery was gentle. She could have hurt me because my power center was exposed, but she walked softly while she shared my form. It wasn't easy for her. I felt her longing for my body. She tires of being nothing but spirit."

Such an interesting insight. I'd never viewed Faery in anything even close to that light. Before I could consider what it might mean, Ysir tottered out from behind an enormous stack of scrolls that threatened to slide to the floor. "Regent. To what do I owe the pleasure? Oh, and you've brought a guest." He peered through shortsighted eyes. "A Witch, is it? Well, well. All are welcome here."

I took in his food-spotted tan robe, matted gray hair, and ink-stained hands and asked, "What happened to your manservant?"

He shrugged. "Hard to say. It's all right, Regent. He doesn't do a lot, anyway."

I could see as much. "I'll assign someone who will take better care of you," I told the ancient Fae librarian and seer.

"Well now, that would be appreciated. I get hungry sometimes, and I'm not the best cook."

Annoyance beat a track through me. Granted, Ysir wasn't the easiest assignment. Crusty and set in his ways, his intransigence grated, but I'd figure out who'd dropped the ball caring for him and assign them to the general kitchens. Washing dishes and peeling vegetables for a decade should take the wind out of their sails.

He'd pinned his rheumy black eyes on me, clearly waiting to see what I needed. "Come on," I invited both him and Dariyah. "I'll make us a pot of tea, and we'll chat."

"That would be lovely." Ysir clasped his hands together. "I have so few visitors."

While we walked to the small kitchen, I raised my mind voice and instructed one of the cooks to send rolls and cheese to the library. If Ysir noticed, he didn't give any indication. Half an hour later, after we'd polished off a pot of herb-infused tea and a light meal, I said, "Dariyah and I are going to search for Titania. She's been gone from Faery for far too long. I've heard rumors she's on a distant world. Do you have any idea which one it might be?"

He leaned toward me and lowered his voice. "I've been so worried about her. She used to come and sit with me, but I can't remember the last time she was here."

I could have jostled his memory and mentioned she'd been missing for half a century. I didn't. "Go on," I urged.

"Only two spots I can think of where she might be," he went on. "Wait a moment. Let me find the proper scrolls." He rose creakily from his seat and wobbled out of the room.

Dariyah placed a hand on my arm. *"Oh my. I feel so sorry for him."*

"I should have paid closer attention."

"You couldn't have known."

I shook my head. *"Not a good enough excuse. This is my realm. Keeping tabs on everyone is part of my job. I've located someone to look after him. They should be here before we leave."*

"Same way the food showed up?" She quirked a brow.

"Same way." I reverted to normal speech as Ysir returned.

He settled into his chair, extracted a scroll from beneath one arm, and unrolled it. "Here." He stabbed the map with a grimy index finger. "Or there." He tapped a second spot. "These are the only two distant worlds that will support life. Although I fail to see why she'd remain in either place for long. Desolate as anything." He clucked his tongue against his teeth.

"Have you been there?" Dariyah asked.

He glanced her way. "Oh my, yes. I've been everywhere. 'Twas I who mapped the universe. Others have come after me. Surely, they have, but I was the first."

A pair of Sidhe trotted smartly into the small room where we sat and bowed to me. "We are here, Regent," one said. Red wings fluttered where she'd pinned them behind her back.

"Aye, willing and ready to take care of our esteemed librarian," the other chimed in. Her wings were a pale, gossamer blue that matched her eyes.

"Thank you for your assistance," I told Ysir. "I will

make a point of visiting more often." I stood; so did Dariyah.

Ysir struggled to his feet. "I would like that, Regent. Please bring your friend with you. Something about her magic is...soothing. Tell Titania I miss her."

"I will. Promise." Tucking Dariyah's hand in mine, I turned to leave. Behind me, I heard one of the Sidhe saying, "Let us draw you a bath, sire. While you bathe, we'll get started cleaning, and—"

"You cannot move anything." Ysir's voice sounded stronger.

"Of course not. We'll clean around everything," the other Sidhe reassured him in a cheerful tone.

"They'll be good for him," Dariyah spoke low.

"I hope so," I murmured. "We'll return to my rooms, and then we'll see if we can't locate the queen."

I could have teleported. It would have saved on questions if anyone saw us together, hand in hand, but I didn't want to hide Dariyah from Faery. Eventually, that bird would come home to roost, and I'd have to face the disconnect between her mixed blood and our covenant. Since we were rewriting it anyway to ensure Oberon couldn't saunter back into Faery and reclaim his throne, we could add a few other bits and pieces.

"It can't be that simple," Dariyah said as we crested the top of the stairs and turned down the hall toward my chambers. It proved she was still residing in my head.

"Why not?"

"Someone made that rule for a reason, the one about it being illegal for differing types of magic wielders to produce children."

I sent magic to open my locked door. It swung inward obligingly, and I stood aside to let her enter ahead of me. Once we were within, I pushed the door shut and strengthened the warding I kept around my domain.

"I believe the person who forwarded that directive—and a whole lot of others that made little sense—was Oberon. Something about non-Fae offended him. Plus, he probably felt threatened by how robust mixed magics could turn out."

Dariyah snorted. "Pfft. He wasn't affronted enough by non-Fae to keep from hiring those like me to spy on you."

"He never viewed hired help as more than part of the landscape. Besides, you didn't live in Faery."

She tugged a chair out from under my small table and dropped into it. "I hate to be a bother, but I need more to eat before we embark on a major journey. I can't imagine it's simple to get to those distant locales."

"Not a bother at all. Let me get what we'll need for the journey, and then we'll stop by the casino. The kitchen can make whatever you'd like."

She frowned. "Why not here?"

I'd been rustling through the cabinet where I keep magical accoutrements. "I'm afraid if we don't make ourselves scarce, something else major will go wrong, and it will be that much harder to leave."

Twisting to face her, I said, "I've always trusted my instincts, and they've been pushing me to hunt for Titania for a long while now. She's the key to ousting Oberon. Why else would he have hidden her away?"

"How do you know she won't support him? Don't mind me. Just playing devil's advocate."

"I'm not 100 percent positive she won't, but I'm willing to take a chance. Besides, she's being held prisoner. It's wrong. Regardless of her sentiments about her consort, I owe it to her to set her free if I can."

I returned to my assortment of herbs and powders and crystals, placing ingredients carefully into containers in a small, flat leather case. Before I was done, Dariyah had gotten up and was leaning over my shoulder. "What are all those things?"

"Mostly items to strengthen my power, make it last longer in case we run into trouble. A few bits and pieces will help if we face unexpected adversaries."

She put her hands on her hips. "Like whom?"

"Oberon must have left underlings watching over Titania. He'd never have chanced her escaping, which she'd be tempted to do."

"Faery seemed to think she was asleep. Does someone drug her whenever she wakes up?"

I shrugged. "Your guess is as good as mine. If fate smiles on us, we'll find out, but I don't want to go all that way unprepared."

"I trust you, which is so rare for me I scarcely recognize what it feels like. Hope I don't live to regret it." She closed her teeth over her lower lip.

"You won't." I'd never meant anything as fervently as those two words. Calling magic, I swept us to the stairwell leading upward into Lady Luck. Dariyah's idea about tanking up on food was a good one. It would replenish my power too, plus who knew when our next meal would be. We didn't linger inhaling generous portions of sushi, rice, and teriyaki balls. Because we were busy eating, talk was sparse.

"You don't have to come," I told her as the meal wound down.

"I know. And I'd be lying if I said I wasn't apprehensive. Since I left Mother, I haven't ventured far from Earth." She stood and stacked her dishes on the tray they'd arrived on. "This is important. You've said you trust your intuition. Mine is screeching I have a role to play, and I'm not going to shirk whatever it is."

I got to my feet, patted my jacket pocket to make certain I still had the leather case, and walked to her side. "I'm not certain how long this will take."

She nodded. "It will go faster if we join our magic."

I felt a shock as she reached for me with her power. The same sense of rightness, of being destined to work as one, rolled through me. Faery had said much the same. That we were fated to come together. I'd thought I knew all the prophecies concerning me. Apparently, I'd been mistaken. If I was missing this one, what else didn't I know about?

I wove a teleport spell using both our skills. My office dropped away, replaced by the gray-black of long-distance travel castings. I had an arm around Dariyah, and she leaned into me. Her eyes were shut; tiny lines scribed around them. She was probably more tired than she'd let on. No matter how careful Faery had been, hosting an entity that powerful had to have been a huge drain. I threaded calming magic around Dariyah, silently urging her to rest while she could.

In far less time than I'd thought possible, the edges of our joint spell developed a gray aspect, which meant we were nearly at our destination. Not sure what to expect, I roused Dariyah. "Almost time," I said. My words were an understatement. The spell broke apart around us, dropping us onto a small island in the middle of a restless sea.

"This can't be right," Dariyah said. "Unless this place is like *Waterworld*."

I recognized the name as a movie, but I'd never seen

it. Stretching seeking strands as far as I could, I searched for a land mass and found one. A quick hop and we stood on a scruffy patch of dirt in the middle of a flock of long-necked golden birds. Startled, they honked and cawed, taking flight, but not going very far from us.

"I don't sense any people here," Dariyah said, "but I could have missed something."

I had no idea if the birds were sentient, but it was worth a shot. Reaching for the nearest one with my mind, I said, *"Forgive the intrusion. We have traveled far and seek Faery's queen. She has been missing for a long while."*

The bird was about the size of a large goose. He turned toward me and angled his head to one side. "And you are?" he squawked.

"Cynwrigg ap Llyr." I bowed.

"And you?" The bird aimed his beady dark eyes at Dariyah.

"My name is Dariyah."

A storm of honking ensued. "Not your true name. Neither is it your only one," the bird intoned. "Faery's queen is not here. We would never be party to an abduction."

My eyebrows shot up. "You know about it?"

"Aye. We do. May luck travel with you." He rose into the air. After a momentary pause, the other birds took flight, tracking after him.

"Of course it's my name," Dariyah sputtered. "It's the only one Mother ever called me."

"It seems like your proper name, but such things can be hidden for the best of reasons," I murmured soothingly and added, "Let's attack one riddle at a time." Marshaling our power, I set coordinates for the other world Ysir had flagged. If we struck out there too, this might be a much shorter trip than I'd anticipated.

The second world was close. It didn't take five minutes before an expanse of violet sky took shape above us. Probably because the other world had been so benign, I'd dropped my guard.

Before the rest of this place finished materializing, we faced a circle of male Fae. I counted five, but others could have been warded and out of sight. I waited until my feet were firmly planted on sandy ground before I said, "I know all of you. You should be in the *Dreaming*."

"The king required our services." The nearest Fae tossed a mane of red hair out of the way.

"Oberon said you'd show up." Another man, this one sporting unevenly trimmed brown curls, displayed a mouthful of teeth. "You're just as poor an excuse for a regent as he said. If you'd been on your toes, you'd have traveled here long ago."

"If you leave now," a third said, "we'll allow it."

"And if we don't?" I kept my tone deceptively mild.

"Plenty of room in the pit with the queen." He chortled, amused by his own joke.

The first Fae rounded on him. "Shut up."

"Why? Numb-nuts here figured things out."

I exchanged a brief glance with Dariyah before testing the waters with this bunch. "All right. We'll clear out as soon as our magic has had a bit of time to recover."

The one who'd labeled me "numb-nuts" thumped my chest with an index finger. "No one said shit about the Witch leaving, mate. We could do with a spot of entertainment. Gets dull around here."

"Oh really, boys?" Dariyah took a step away from my side and then another. "You think you want me. Come and get me. This should be a hoot."

I'd planned on something more subtle. Sneaking about under the guise of needing time to rebuild my magic. Dariyah was more of an in-your-face mage. It was one of many things I was coming to love about her.

"Cyn?" she jabbed me with magic.

That's the thing about working with a partner. You back their plays. "We got this," I told her and tossed my magic wide open.

CHAPTER FIFTEEN, DARIYAH

So I was the entertainment committee, huh? We'd see about that, and not in a way this crew of jokers would appreciate. Even without Cyn's magic, I could eat them for breakfast and spit them into the wind. Together, we'd make the horny upstarts sorry they'd gotten out of bed this morning.

I'd done a cursory search and hadn't turned up any more Fae, but neither had I found Titania. If her presence was that closely guarded, others could be in hiding as well. Best not take anything for granted. I had no idea what all the powders and potions in Cyn's pouch were about. I'd always done my magic *au naturel*, using the gifts living within me. Except for the occasions I resorted to a knife.

It was how Mother had taught me. If I'd been raised

in Faery, I might have learned differently.

No. If I'd grown up in Faery, the growing up part never would have happened. Anger at the injustice of it added fuel to my willingness to flatten the Fae who thought they'd dick with me. No one laid a hand on me without my permission. No one.

"Come and get you, darling?" The red-haired Fae leered at me. "With pleasure."

"Feel free to give it a shot." I added honey to my words, and the stupid twit fell for it.

I waited until he was close enough the bulge in his pants was almost touching me before loosing a stream of magic at his crotch. Not only mine, but the mingled power Cyn and I produced. The Fae screeched as if he'd been skinned alive and grabbed his distended cock as he hopped from foot to foot.

"What did you do?" he howled.

I dusted my hands together. "Nothing much. You never needed that body part, so you won't mind watching it wither and rot away."

"He won't live that long," Cynwrigg snarled, his hands a blur as he pounded power into a noose that wound around the Fae's neck like a homing pigeon.

"Creative." I gave Cyn a thumbs up and instructed the rope to tighten, but oh so slowly. The bastard had been ready to rape me. He deserved to suffer before his pathetic excuse for a life was snuffed out.

The other four leapt toward us. I'm sure they made a bunch of bad assumptions, the first being that my supposed Witchy powers were inferior. Too bad for them Oberon's whole ethnic superiority propaganda gig had been woefully shortsighted. I'd met some extremely strong Witches in my time.

"Dibs on them." I sprang through the air toward the two nearest me. Their magic collided with mine forming a crackling mess of a blaze. I hacked through it and kicked one in the nuts. He dropped like a stone, screeching.

Sheesh. Men. They were such a bunch of pussies.

I caught glimpses of Cynwrigg out of the corners of my eyes. A blade had materialized from somewhere, glowing with power as he leapt and swung and parried. It shouldn't have surprised me he'd been well-trained in military arts, but it did. I'd figured everyone in Faery only fought with magic.

I know better than to divert my attention—for anything. Knowing and doing aren't the same, though. While I was admiring Cyn's skills, my other selected victim circled round behind me and grabbed my arms. Something like an executioner's hood dropped over my head. It smelled musty and reeked of fear. I felt sorry for the person who'd worn it last. Power oozed from it. If I'd been anything other than what I am, it might have slowed me down. A quick assessment gave me what I needed to defeat its insidious folds.

Meanwhile, the dick who'd snatched my arms had moved a hand to one of my breasts. His hard-on prodded my ass. I'd been humoring him while I built a spell to rip the stupid hood to shreds. No more. Kicking my head back, I rammed his face hard enough to break his nose. Bones shattered with a satisfying *crack*.

It had the desired effect. He dropped his hold on me as if I'd suddenly become too hot to handle. The analogy amused me—and gave me an idea. I fed earth and fire to the hood. I knew better than to try to rip it off. He'd spelled it to remain in place, but he couldn't do much about me destroying it. Smoke rose, along with the stench of burning hair. My hair, but it was a small price. I added water to my casting, instructing it to beat back the flames.

"Damn it, Dariyah." I heard Cyn as if from a great distance away.

Ripping and tearing battered my ears as the enchanted hood was gutted from the crown of my head downward. Blackened shards fluttered to the ground all around me. Spinning, I nailed my assailant with more than enough magic to flatten him, and then I pinned him to the earth with burning cords designed to erode his flesh.

Two could play this game, and he'd pissed me off.

Cyn was tucking a glowing blade back into the pouch he'd put together back in Faery. Magical to its core, the length of glowing metal was capable of many forms, from the longsword he'd fought with to whatever he'd used to slice the hood open. Handy it got small enough to tuck away.

I wanted one just like it. Even though I relied on magic, I was clever with knives.

"We concede," the one I'd booted in the nuts croaked. "Free us, and we'll return to the *Dreaming* and—"

"The fuck you will," Cyn snarled. "Where is Titania?"

A sly look stole over his twisted features. "After I show you, then you'll release me to the *Dreaming*."

"Perhaps."

I opened my mouth to lodge a protest, but snapped it shut. Cyn was hedging. We could find the queen on our own, but it would be simpler if we didn't have to waste time hunting. A quick glance confirmed the greeting party weren't a threat any longer. The one with the noose around his neck lay comatose and twitching. Cop-a-Feel dude was slowly turning into a smoldering sacrifice. The two Cynwrigg had worked over had a dazed look, as if their minds were gone. The only one on his feet was the one whose nose I'd broken, and he'd shifted his focus from everyone being released to saving his own hide.

No loyalty among blackguards and thieves.

The earth beneath my feet began to hum. "Cyn!" I shouted and stamped the packed dirt. Alarm sluiced through me. Fighting people was one thing, but this felt like an assault from the heart of this world. A long, jagged crack formed amid hissing and popping as the earth pulled apart.

It was a lot like the rift I'd healed for Faery, but that one had been static, not reshaping itself by the minute. I experimented with a thin strip of the same mix of power I'd used before. Something snatched it and chucked it back in my face, a giant hand reaching out and slapping me. My ears rang, my eyes watered, and I thanked my common sense for starting small. A gutsier exploratory sequence could have seriously injured me.

Cyn vaulted to my side and grabbed a hand. "On my count of three," he said.

"What are we doing?"

"Jumping." He jerked his chin at the widening gap.

My words about trusting him rose to the fore. I did, but was it enough to leap into the crack? What if this whole thing had been some elaborately staged charade aimed at trapping me? What if—? I ripped my negativity out by its roots. This was Cynwrigg. We were partners, allies. He'd never hurt me. I'd tested his intent from here to Sunday and not found anything that gave me pause.

"Dariyah?" His gold-and-silver eyes bored into me. "I

cannot leave you here alone. You must come with me. And we have to do this now."

It was one of those fish-or-cut-bait moments. Either I accepted he knew what he was doing, or I had no business being here at all. I'd come this far; now wasn't a time to backpedal. If I said, fuck no I wasn't jumping into that pulsing hole, he wouldn't go, either. And we'd lose something I had no name for.

Even beyond whatever he was after in the trench, he'd realize I didn't have enough faith in him to follow his lead. I hadn't obeyed anyone's instructions since leaving Mother, and he probably knew it.

My heart was pounding hard, my mouth dust-dry as I gritted, "Let's go."

He didn't waste another second. When I looked at the ground instead of him, I understood why. The gash, which had been expanding, was definitely moving in the opposite direction. It had torn open, but now it was closing.

Crap. Had I dithered too long? Were we too late?

Darkness enveloped us. A dusky shroud shot through with magic burned and prickled as I fell through it. Unlike a teleport spell, we fell in real time. Seconds ticked past, and then minutes. The only constant was the pressure of Cyn's hand around mine. I tightened the weave where our magic was joined. Bands of light broke the unremitting black, becoming more frequent as we continued. The longer we persisted, the surer I was we weren't falling at all.

That had to be it. The whole thing, rift and all, was illusion. Cyn had recognized it, and— All my conjecture was stupid. He was right here, front and center. "Where are we going?" I asked.

He chuckled. "Wondered when you'd get around to inquiring. By the way, thanks for trusting me. You almost didn't." He traded my hand for wrapping an arm around my shoulders. "The power eddying around us is Titania's. It's been a long while, but I'd recognize it anywhere."

"She opened a path for us?"

"It sure as hell wasn't that ridiculous pack of jokers up there."

"How much farther? Do you know?"

He shook his head. I felt rather than saw the motion. "It only feels like we're traveling. She's being cautious, and I don't blame her."

Yeah, neither did I. "You don't suppose her jailers, um..."

"They wouldn't have dared lay a hand on her." Cyn picked up the drift of my unspoken question about rape. "She might have been a prisoner, but she was still their queen."

"How does that work?" I asked. "Oberon sort of abdicated, and—"

"Except he didn't, which is why we have to rework

the covenant. Get ready. We're nearly at an end to this enchantment."

He hadn't been kidding. The darkness exploded with a resounding *thwack*. In its place was a whimsical structure. I'd have called it a castle if it were larger. Built from uneven chunks of what looked like quartz and large timbers, it spread before me in a scene right out of *Grimm's Fairytales*, complete with a miniature moat, a drawbridge, turrets, and a portcullis.

A sharp intake of breath radiated dismay. I looked at Cyn. "You know this place?"

He nodded. "I do, indeed. This is the original version of Dubrova castle, but on a much smaller scale." Jets of seeking magic flowed from his raised hands, and his worried expression deepened, adding lines to his high forehead.

"Talk to me," I urged.

"The only thing holding this place together is Titania's magic, and it's fading. Damn Oberon's eyes. I hope we got here in time."

I didn't require further explanation for that statement. Absent something like what we did to the greeting party, Fae don't die, but we do fade to nothing but spirit. Sometimes, the weight of millennia is enough to push us over the edge. Sometimes, the pull of the *Dreaming* with its idyllic pathways is too much to resist. Mother had said it fulfilled all your dreams, ensured you wanted for nothing. It had sounded enticing and scary as fuck. Not the being there, but the prying yourself away.

I sprinted across the drawbridge after Cyn. He barked a couple of words, and the portcullis creaked upward. We could have teleported through it, but this was faster. I scanned the still waters of the moat, half expecting to see serpents, but none reared their heads. We'd reached the castle's imposing front door. Crafted of the same wood as the structure's timbers, it had been inscribed with runes. I recognized a few and shook my head. "We have to erase those, or she'll never be able to cross." To be on the safe side, I scoured the door with destructive magic. Maybe two-thirds of the runes glowed an angry red before being absorbed by the wood.

"You're efficient." Cyn grinned approvingly.

"Eh. I try. Obliterated the worst of them. The others shouldn't pose problems."

"I have faith in Titania's power," he said, "unless she's given up hope."

"She hasn't," I said firmly. "She opened a path for us. If she'd truly renounced all faith, she wouldn't have cared who was here."

"I hope you're right." Cyn paused in a generous hall inlaid with marble. How in the hell had whoever built this place come by quartz and marble and hardwood? From what I'd seen of this world, none of those elements were native to it, but then I'd only viewed a very small portion.

He said, "This way," about the same time a wraith glided toward us. Lush royal robes in blue and silver hung on her emaciated frame. White hair spilled to the floor around a sharp-boned face.

"Cynwrigg. Is that really you, or one more flight of fancy on my part?" Titania hung back. The hand she extended shook as power pulsed weakly from it.

"It's really me." He rushed forward and fell to his knees before his queen. "Thank the goddess I didn't arrive too late."

A tear formed in one of her eyes and crept down her wrinkled cheek. "Get up," she said gruffly. When he did, she threw herself into his arms, and he held her, crooning softly. If I'd been in her shoes, a prisoner for half a century, I'd have sobbed my heart out at the specter of imminent rescue.

Not Titania. She let go of Cyn after maybe two minutes and straightened, locking gazes with him. "You should have come years ago."

He inclined his head. "Aye, my lady, I know. Let me get you out of here."

It might have been a trick of the light, but she was standing taller, not looking as frail or pallid. "You killed my guards, most of them. I felt some pass, and the others are weakening." She fisted one veined hand.

"Good. I didn't believe it possible. They were some of Oberon's best warriors once."

"Pfft." I tossed my head. "They were nothing but rotters and cowards. It was a pleasure to—"

I wouldn't have believed Titania could move so quickly, but one minute she was next to Cyn and the next she stood in front of me poking and prodding with strong magic that stung my skin. The singed places in my scalp vibrated unpleasantly, but I held myself still beneath her scrutiny.

"How is this possible?" She fixed me with eyes of molten gold.

I didn't flinch beneath her gaze. "How is what possible?" I considered adding "my lady," but I wasn't part of Faery, and so I chose not to.

"You're Auril's daughter. Do not deny it."

"Why would I?" I shot back. "I'm proud of Mother. She could have sacrificed me. She didn't."

Titania ran a hand from my ruined hair down one cheek, letting it rest on my shoulder briefly. "You're supposed to be dead. Oberon inferred as much, but I can add it to the pile of his other half truths."

Not sure where she was going with this, I said, "Mother and I ran for five years. It took that long for *your* people"—I stressed the your part—"to leave us in peace."

"Where is she, child?" Titania's voice was soft, too soft.

Suspicion raked me. "I will not tell anyone where Mother is."

Cyn had walked behind me. "Auril is your mother?" Incredulity scored his words.

I twisted to glance his way. "I just said as much. The Fae only care about rounding her up and ending her."

"Not such an easy task, the rounding up and ending. She's the Queen of Air and Darkness," Cyn murmured.

"The who?" Confusion scoured me, and I shifted my attention back to Titania. "Mother was royalty? Did that play into our headlong flight to escape Faery?"

"Oh my, child. She never told you." Titania frowned, her white brows forming a single line.

"Told me what? Come on, both of you. Whatever this is, spit it out." What had Cyn called Mother? The Queen of Air and Darkness... An impressive title, but not one that had ever fallen from Mother's lips. Not in my presence.

"Auril was—is—my only sister. I'd thought her dead centuries ago." The queen's eyes narrowed as she repeated her earlier question, "You know where she is, don't you?"

I nodded slowly, looking for a catch, a trap door that would swallow Mother and me if I weren't cautious.

"Use a truth spell," Titania urged. "Test my words.

You'll find them accurate."

A flicker of amazement in Cyn's eyes told me how rare her invitation was. She was queen of Faery. No one questioned her. I should take her word—and Cyn's—but I had to be certain, so I draped a soft weave around the queen's head and shoulders and urged, "Tell me about Mother."

"She is my sister, my older sister. Many sisters hate one another, but Auril and I were heart-sisters. I loved her more than anyone else. When she came to me and told me she was pregnant and had to flee, I was devastated. I searched and searched but couldn't come up with a way to hold her in Faery. Already, others suspected her condition."

"I remember," Cyn cut in, his voice deep, warm, and steady.

"As do I, all too well," Titania went on. "Oberon suspected something was up, but he never put two and two together until after the babe were born. I did manage that part. Auril intended to leave right away, but I didn't want her to be alone through her pregnancy. So much could have gone wrong. She and I found a deep cavern, straddling the boundary betwixt Faery and Earth. We swathed it with our combined magic. Faery helped keep our secret until the birth. My sister was weaker than she'd expected, so she remained with Faery and me for a fortnight before fleeing with her child."

It was the first account of my birth I'd heard that hadn't come from Mother. I'd always believed I was born on an alien world, one we'd abandoned as soon as Mother was strong enough to run some more. I dismantled my truth casting and looked into Titania's ancient eyes. "You know who my father is."

She nodded. "Aye, but such is for Auril to tell you, not me. Shall we go to her?"

I wanted to ask for time to consider everything that could go sideways, except we didn't have any. We needed to leave this spot right away before Oberon rode in with a vigilante regiment.

"My turn to share your thoughts," Cyn murmured. "I agree. We should have been gone as soon as Titania joined us."

I sucked in a breath and took a chance. Everything Titania said about Mother had passed the test of my truth weave, and—

"Child." Titania's stern tone broke into my shillyshallying. "I shall restore Auril to her rightful spot in Faery. Together, she and I can bar Oberon from our land forever. She is queen of the dark court, while I command the light one."

"So, that wasn't idle legend?" Cyn inquired.

"No legends are idle. We maintained the same dark-and-light-court arrangement as the Sidhe. They allied with us, and we joined their festivities as well. It always rankled Oberon, and he never missed an opportunity to make Auril's life difficult. Shall we?"

I led the way through the door I'd prepped so she could pass beneath its lintels and built a spell as quickly as I could. If I stopped to think, I might lose my nerve. This was sounding too good to be true—the part about Mother getting a pass to return to her rightful place.

I've never trusted fortune when she walks across my grave bearing gifts, though. The other shoe would drop, but I had no idea when it would happen. In the meantime, my intuition about accompanying Cynwrigg on this quest had been dead accurate. I was here for reasons stretching far beyond me, and I'd see things through.

Eventually the enchantment powering my not-so-chance meeting with Titania would burn itself to cinders. What would emerge from the ashes?

Patience, my inner critic noted dryly. *No turning back now.*

You've reached the end of *Court of Rogues*. Misfits and Magick is a serial that's continued in *Midnight Court*. While *Court of Rogues* is fresh in your mind, please take a moment and leave a review. They mean so much to authors. Doesn't have to be fancy. A line or two will do. Curious what happens next? Read on for the prologue to *Midnight Court*.

BOOK DESCRIPTION: MIDNIGHT COURT

Urban fantasy and slow burn romance wrapped into a serial that will keep you up reading long into the night.

Strange bedfellows rock worlds.

My days as Faery's reluctant regent have crashed and burned. Either I left the land to rot in a squalid soup of broken promises, or I destroyed her enemies one by one. No choice there. Not really. I'd known some of those "enemies" since childhood, which was centuries ago. They say familiarity breeds contempt. In my case it bred sorrow as I consigned Fae who'd been friends to eternal destruction and fed them to the land.

Dariyah, the Witch-who-wasn't-one, crossed my path for reasons I'm still figuring out. Her long-lost mother presided over one of Faery's many dirty secrets, the Midnight Court. Some like to believe Fae blood is pure. It's not. The Sidhe and us are joined at the hip, and the Midnight Court was once a living symbol of our bond.

I'll fight to maintain a magical world that's open to all. If I'm quick, ruthless, I might beat Oberon at his own game. Sly bastard that he is, he still holds the link to Faery. If I can't wrest it from him, the land—my land—will wither and fade.

MIDNIGHT COURT, PROLOGUE, AURIL

uril clung to patterns, to sameness. She had little choice; consistency made the impossible bearable. For the first couple of centuries, she'd kept track of time passing, but it was depressing. So many days, weeks, years had dripped past, time no longer mattered. This wasn't like prison because it never ended. And it sure as hell wasn't anything like the *Dreaming*, a retreat anticipating your every whim. No *Dreaming* for her. Not ever. She'd always viewed herself as a loner, self-contained. Until she was faced with endless isolation. Then she realized she'd been deluding herself all along.

Once she'd been the Queen of Air and Darkness. But a queen requires subjects, and they were no more. She'd moved on, leaving the shell of queendom behind. The court she'd presided over was no more, erased by absence and the passage of time.

Too late to do anything about it. It had been too late for an exceedingly long while. Besides, it wasn't as if she'd had options. Not really. By the time she'd stumbled onto this world hidden from all others, the dice were tossed. No going back. She had a toddler to raise. Young as Dariyah was, power shimmered around her like a veil, spilling from her hair, her eyes, her fingertips in an endless stream of possibilities.

The child was beauty incarnate, with a sweet and inquisitive soul. Bright, curious, inspired, she more than made up for everything Auril had left behind. She'd seen some of the future unfold in her glass. More in various pools. Regardless, she'd viewed enough to understand her child was a critical element, an instrument meant to shape the future.

Her sister, Titania, wasn't one to put much stock in prophecies. She'd talked until no more words came, urging Auril to look past the life that had taken root in her womb. Many magic-wielders had walked in her footsteps, had taken the necessary steps to deal with mixed-breed offspring. Those had been Titania's words: deal with it. Innocuous enough, except in this instance dealing meant death. Auril couldn't have done that any more than she could have cut off an arm or a leg. The child was destined to be. Its call from the beyond—an amorphous spot where souls resided—was so strong, it had swept her up in its urgency.

And so she'd fled from both Fae and Sidhe, from her duties to the Midnight Court, knowing there'd be fallout. And there had been. Her energy was a lynchpin keeping Faery whole. Between her and her sister, they'd balanced the dark and light sides of magic, feeding Faery and keeping her hale and hearty.

She'd asked questions a million different ways, working to tease out if her worst fears for Faery had come to pass. No answers had been forthcoming until a few days ago when a scrying attempt blew up in her face, showering her with water and leaving her with a deeply uncomfortable premonition the world she'd abandoned was finally unraveling at the seams.

Auril wrapped her arms around her bent knees and slumped against the rocky wall behind her. Should she return? After all this time, no one would remember the whispered rumors about a forbidden pregnancy. Eh, the ancient librarian, Ysir, might, but he'd been well on his way to madness long before she left.

Obscuring the relationship between Fae and Sidhe was another dirty little secret she'd been part of. The two lines sprang from common roots, and their power blended perfectly, creating awe inspiring magic. Remembering its perfection still stole her breath. The multi-hued strands of talent had filled her with joy as they knitted into various spells, but the same blended power terrified Oberon. Perhaps because it existed outside the realm of his control. Regardless of his motives, he'd done everything in his considerable power to squelch every juncture where Fae and Sidhe came together.

Her court, the Midnight Court, had been a center-piece for combined magic. After Oberon ordered it disbanded, She and Titania had moved it underground. For a long while, she'd been certain Oberon would find out and put a stop to it, but he had a lazy streak a mile wide, and he'd never dug too deep. Nighttime festivals where everyone danced beneath Faery's twinkling stars flourished, until the land switched to perpetual daylight.

She'd been certain it was Oberon's backhanded way of punishing them, but Titania assured her that wasn't it at all. They'd taken care to erase revelers' memories of those enchanted gatherings, so a snitch in the crowd couldn't have been the problem. Hell, they'd even silenced the nightingales. She hugged her arms tighter around her legs and smiled as pleasant recollections of warm, lazy nights buffeted her. Rather like a cross between Beltane and Lughnasadh, there'd been plenty of laughter and sex and trading of all sorts.

Joy was a powerful motivator, a heady inspiration.

How long could she live on memories? The question curled her lip into a sneer. Apparently, forever. Faery's gates were no longer open to her, the Midnight Court long shuttered.

A breathy sigh rocked her, followed by another. Feeling sorry for herself wasn't her style. She'd get over this rough patch. Soon. Nothing had changed except she'd allowed herself to long for the impossible.

Everything that happened in this remote outpost occurred—or didn't—because of things she did. Exercising that level of control should have been satisfying, but it wasn't. Letting her daughter go—forcing her to leave was closer to the mark—was one of the hardest things she'd ever done. It meant she'd be alone forever, but what kind of life had she condemned Dariyah to? Auril squeezed her eyes shut tight. She'd done the best she could. Ensured the child lived and flourished, so the power within her could find its potential.

More drill sergeant than Mother, she'd trained the girl's magic. Taught her to harness her raw ability to protect herself. And she'd hidden her true name. Names have incalculable power. So long as Dariyah didn't know hers, no one could wrest if from her. Auril's guts twisted into a physical ache. She'd followed her daughter, scrying her location and some of her activities over the eons they'd been separated. Each glimpse was a two-edged sword, mixing relief with a pervasive sorrow. She'd never lay eyes on her daughter again. She should have come to terms with that reality long since.

Should have.

Dariyah was alive. Knowing she'd survived should have been enough, but it wasn't. Many a night Auril tossed and turned. Sleep was elusive because she longed to wrap her arms around Dariyah and feel the beat of her heart. Seeing her in visions, in imagery that ebbed and flowed, wasn't the same. Not even close.

Pushing upright from spot she'd been crouched near her favorite scrying pool, she strode toward a cave. She visited it every afternoon at just this time. It was one of the patterns she'd maintained no matter what else was going on. Not that anything ever happened to disturb her routine. Sometimes, she wished something would, and then she offered up prayers to the goddess and said she hadn't meant it.

Monotony and boredom were preferable to unknown elements infiltrating her tiny corner of the universe.

Light flickered and flashed off the walls of a rounded crystalline cave. The lights came from the core of this world and bounced off the surface of a large, subterranean lake. Unlike Faery, this place wasn't inclined to talk. Strange since they were the only two sentient entities here. Auril had moved past lonely a few centuries ago, but the land endured. Silent, stoic, and ostensibly without needs of its own.

She'd visited the cave so often, she'd worn a path in the rocky dirt. Following it, she walked to the spot she always sat. Energy converged just there and made her future-seeing easier. Not that she had to conserve power. Nothing to use it for here, but she was cautious by nature. Just because no one had breached the borders of her lair didn't mean it couldn't happen.

At least she was past the worst of her spate of self-pity. She reminded herself nothing had altered except her focus. Looking backward wasn't productive. All it did was make her sad. She shook herself from head to toe before settling on her haunches on damp sand a handspan from the murky water. By all the gods and goddesses, she was still a queen and she damned well needed to act like one. Her title had been conferred by Danu herself in a joint ceremony with Titania.

It had been very hush-hush, and Oberon hadn't been invited. The old geezer had been livid when he broke through Danu's barrier shielding the ritual from plain view. And even more outraged when the goddess sent him packing. The memory still brought a smile.

Auril twisted her mouth into a grimace. How Titania had continued to stand by her consort after all his shenanigans was tough to understand, but it was a sore topic. She and her sister never discussed him, for obvious reasons. If she'd been the one shackled to

Oberon, she'd have cut off his dick and muffled his smart mouth with spells long ago.

The thought turned the grimace into a vicious grin. If she ever walked beneath Faery's skies again, the first thing she'd do would be to hang Oberon in effigy in the Midnight Court. Voodoo borrowed a page from her court, and she'd make the noose feel so authentic, the king of Faery would go running for his spell book in search of an antidote.

Sucking air to the very bottom of her lungs, she blew it out and then repeated the action a few times to center herself. A low hum began at the base of her spine and flowed upward, telling her the day's scrying session was well in hand. She preferred the outdoor pond she'd been settled next to, but power resided within the cave, and it fueled her efforts. With her arms extended in front of her and power arcing from her fingertips, she shut her earth eyes and switched to her psychic view.

The surface of the lake developed waves that swished back and forth before parting to form something that reminded her of a stage. At first it remained empty, it's polished boards glistening gold in the odd light from the cave. Figures ebbed and flowed, not clear enough to make out beyond there being three of them. Auril waited. She'd been here before. The vision would speak to her in its own time.

Keep breathing, she instructed, certain of her magic,

of her innate ability. Out of all her skills, her seer ability had never failed. The edges of the vision started curling in on themselves. Her eyes widened as shock punched her in the guts. She sprang to her feet, hands still outstretched and sent a jolt of enchantment dead center into the fading tableau.

"Reveal," she shouted. "I command you."

The vision should have shaped right up. It didn't, but at least it stopped collapsing. "That's right," Auril crooned. "Show me your truth."

Naught about today was panning out as she'd expected. Why should this be any different? She'd anticipated a gradual unfolding of a series of images for her to decrypt. The messages that came to her this way were never clear-cut.

Nothing slow and steady here, though. One minute, the perimeter circling the stage was about to implode, the next Titania, Dariyah, and a man who looked familiar burst into view. Heads together, the three of them were talking among themselves, features carved into anxious expressions.

Titania flinched, and then straightened and turned. If she'd been in the cave, she'd have been staring dead into Auril's eyes. "Sister"—she tossed her head in a gesture so familiar, it smote Auril—"We shall be there soon."

The tableau burst from the inside outward in a blaze

of reds and violets, leaving her staring at motes of light. Auril rubbed her eyes, not trusting anything. How had Titania sensed her across worlds and time? What was Dariyah doing with her sister?

What in the unholy fuck had happened since she'd last seen Dariyah in a vision? Her daughter had been in some kind of arcade playing cards with cat hairs stuck to her clothing and a human in thrall.

About the only answer that rose to the surface was the male Fae's identity. He was Cynwrigg ap Llyr, first in line for Faery's throne. Did his appearance with Titania mean Oberon was gone?

"A queen can dream," she muttered, breaking the silence stretching through the cavern. More truths marched across her mind. Dariyah must have told Titania where to find her. It was the only way her sister could have discovered this out-of-the-way realm.

Titania had said "we." Presumably, it meant all of them would arrive soon, the implication punched her in the guts. Her heart beat like a trip hammer; excitement raced through her. Dariyah would actually be here next to her, in her arms where she could pat her, touch her. Stroke hair out of her face and make all the maternal noises she'd avoided for fear of spoiling the child.

She's not a child anymore. Her implacable inner voice brought her up short. *Better to love and accept the woman she's grown into.*

Her mouth twisted into a wry grin. Grand advice. Who knew how it would play out? Dariyah's magic existed in a class of its own. What had she done with her talents? Had the time come for her to stroll into Faery and take her rightful place amongst its leaders? Auril hadn't disclosed that part of her future-seeing to her daughter. She'd told her to steer clear of Faery because her mixed blood could spell her death—until she came into her own and was strong enough to claim her birthright.

Auril sank into a crouch, kneeling next to the dark waters of the lake. Its surface had quieted, but not for long. Once again, she extended her hands and bounced jolts of lightning off the water's surface. "Show me the future," she intoned. "Do it now. No more games."

Enchantment sheeted from her, marrying her mind to the universe. If her viewing of Titania had been true —and it almost had to be—worlds had shifted on their axes. She'd shed one skin when she left Faery. Maybe it was time to shed the one she'd worn ever since.

Breath burst from her, and she didn't make the slightest effort to mute her triumph. A celebration might be premature, but she was done pussyfooting around and playing nice with destiny. If the Queen of Air and Darkness was about to rise from her self-imposed crypt, she was more than ready to make it happen with her daughter and sister by her side.

The three of them should be unbreakable. She'd seen it often enough in dreams and visions. "Not should be, will be." She breathed the words and turned her attention to her nascent spell twisting the lake's dark water to her purposes.

ABOUT THE AUTHOR

Ann Gimpel is a USA Today bestselling author. A life-long aficionado of the unusual, she began writing speculative fiction a few years ago. Since then her short fiction has appeared in many webzines and anthologies. Her longer books run the gamut from urban fantasy to paranormal romance. Once upon a time, she nurtured clients. Now she nurtures dark, gritty fantasy stories that push hard against reality. When she's not writing, she's in the backcountry getting down and dirty with her camera. She's published over 80 books to date, with several more planned for 2020 and beyond. A husband, grown children, grandchildren, and wolf hybrids round out her family.

Keep up with her at www.anngimpel.com or http://anngimpel.blogspot.com

If you enjoyed what you read, get in line for special offers and pre-release special reads. Newsletter Signup!

Blood and Sorcery

Blood and Illusion

Demon Assassins

Witch's Bounty

Witch's Bane

Witches Rule

Dragon Heir

Dragon's Call

Dragon's Blood

Dragon's Heir

Dragon Lore

Highland Secrets

To Love a Highland Dragon

Dragon Maid

Dragon's Dare

Dragon Fury

Earth Reclaimed

Earth's Requiem

Earth's Blood

Earth's Hope

Elemental Witch

Timespell

Time's Curse

Time's Hostage

Gatekeeper

Shadow Reaper

Rebel Reaper

Untamed Reaper

GenTech Rebellion

Winning Glory

Honor Bound

Claiming Charity

Loving Hope

Keeping Faith

Ice Dragon

Feral Ice

Cursed Ice

Primal Ice

Magick and Misfits (Fall and Winter 2020)

Court of Rogues

Midnight Court

Court of the Fallen

Court of Destiny

Rubicon International

Garen

Lars

Soul Dance

Tarnished Beginnings

Tarnished Legacy

Tarnished Prophecy

Tarnished Journey

Soul Storm

Dark Prophecy

Dark Pursuit

Dark Promise

Underground Heat

Roman's Gold

Wolf Born

Blood Bond

Wolf Clan Shifters

Alice's Alphas

Megan's Mates

Sophie's Shifters

Wylde Magick

Gemstone

Lion's Lair

Unbalanced

STANDALONE BOOKS

Branded, That Old Black Magic Romance (paranormal romance)

Edge of Night (short story collection, paranormal and horror)

Grit is a 4-Letter Word (nonfiction)

Heart's Flame (post-apocalyptic romance)

Icy Passage (science fiction romance)

Marked by Fortune (post-apocalyptic coming of age story)

Melis's Gambit (historical paranormal romance)

Midnight Magic (paranormal romance)

Red Dawn (post-apocalyptic paranormal romance)

Shadow Play (historical paranormal romance)

Shadows in Time (Highland time travel romance)

Since We Fell (contemporary romance)

Warin's War (paranormal romance)